LEONARDO SCIASCIA was born in 1921 at Racalmuto, near Agrigento, in southwestern Sicily. He taught in a primary school, trained as a lawyer, and published his first novel, *The Day of the Owl*, in 1961. He became a full-time writer with the publication of his historical novel, *Council of Egypt*, in 1963. He also took an active part in politics, with a seat in parliament first as a Communist, later as a radical; he was a Euro-MP in 1979. He died in Palermo in 1989, leaving a rich and varied opus including novels, short stories and very trenchant reportage on his native Sicily. "Out of his curious Sicilian experience," wrote Gore Vidal, "Sciascia made a literature that is not quite like anything else ever done by a European."

Leonardo Sciascia

CANDIDO

or

A DREAM DREAMED IN SICILY

*Translated from the Italian
by Adrienne Foulke*

THE HARVILL PRESS
LONDON

First published in Great Britain 1982 by
Carcanet New Press Limited

This paperback edition published 1995 by
The Harvill Press
84 Thornhill Road
London N1 1RD

Copyright © 1977 by Giulio Einaudi editore s.p.a.

English translation © 1979 by
Harcourt Brace and Jovanovich, Inc.

A CIP catalogue record for this title is available
from the British Library

ISBN 1 84046 026 7

Printed and bound in Great Britain by
Butler & Tanner Ltd, Frome and London

About the place and the night of Candido
Munafò's birth, and about the reason for which
he was given the name Candido
3

About how the lawyer Munafò began to doubt
that he was the father of Candido, and about
the troubles that ensued from this
8

About the departure and the return of Hamlet,
and about what befell the lawyer Munafò
deservedly and Candido undeservedly
13

About the solitude of the lawyer Munafò,
and about that of Candido
16

About how Candido arrived at the state of being
an almost total orphan, and about the risk
he ran of emigrating to Helena, Montana
21

About the compassionate censure of which Candido
was the object on the part of the General, relatives,
and virtually the entire city, and about his behavior
when he became aware of it
26

About the concern of the General and of Concetta for Candido's education; and about the General's decision to give him, as in bygone days, a tutor
31

About the things of which Candido and the Archpriest used to talk, and about the vexation this caused the General
36

About the power that Candido did not know he had over his nearest of kin; and about his impressions and his actions when he found out that he had it
42

About the mysterious crime, the author of which Candido and the Archpriest happened to discover; and about the condemnation both received from the entire city, and the Archpriest from the hierarchy as well
48

About the attempt the ex-Archpriest made to dedicate himself to cultivating his own garden, and Candido his land; and about their disappointments therefrom
53

About the journey that Candido and Don Antonio made to Lourdes; and about the good that it did them both
59

*About the love for women, and for one woman,
by which Candido was seized; and about what
Don Antonio had to say to him in this regard*
64

*About the Communism of Candido and of Don
Antonio; and about the discussions that they
had with each other and with comrades*
69

*About how the General became enraged with Candido
and Paola; and about Paola's going to live in
Candido's house, and the consequent
flight of Concetta*
75

*About the warnings Candido received from the
Party; and about how the first steps were taken
to build a case against him*
78

*About the life that Candido led between home,
the country, and the Party; and about the
proposal that was made to him and that
he did not accept*
81

*About the arduous inquiry that the Party
conducted to identify Foma Fomitch; and about
the conversations Candido and Don Antonio
had about this personage*
88

*About the disappearance of Paola, and about
what she forgot to take with her*
93

*About the decision that Candido made to
free himself of his land, and to travel, and
about how his relatives went to great pains
to set him free*
99

*About the colloquy that Candido had with a
judge and a psychiatrist, and about the judgment
of mental incompetency that followed from it*
105

*About the party that Candido's relatives gave him
as a reward for his behavior before the judge and
the doctors; and about the troubles that befell
his relatives as a consequence of that party*
109

*About the travels of Candido and Francesca,
and about their long sojourn in Turin*
113

*About the trips of Candido and Francesca to Paris,
and about their decision to settle there*
118

*About the correspondence between Candido and
Don Antonio; and about Don Antonio's
journey to Paris*
122

*About the meeting of Candido with his mother,
and about the evening they spent together, and
about how, that evening, Candido managed
to feel happy*
126

Author's Note
133

CANDIDO

or

A DREAM DREAMED IN SICILY

*About the place and the night of Candido
Munafò's birth, and about the reason for which
he was given the name Candido*

Candido Munafò was born on the night of July 9–10, 1943, in a grotto that opened, wide and deep, at the foot of a hillside of olive trees. Nothing was easier than to be born in a grotto or in a stable that summer and especially that night in Sicily, as it was fought over by the American Seventh Army under General Patton, the British Eighth Army under General Montgomery, the Hermann Goering Division, and several skeletal, almost invisible Italian regiments. It was on that very night, while the island's skies were ominously illuminated by multicolored Bengal lights and its cities were plowed by bombs, that the armies of Patton and Montgomery disembarked.

There was, then, no supernatural or premonitory sign in Candido Munafò's being born in a grotto; or in the fact that that grotto lay in the district of Serradifalco, "mountain of the falcon," a place from which to take flight—predatory flight; or, even less, in the fact that throughout that night now reddish, now white-hot rockets lighted the sky, and that the sky echoed with a vast metallic chirping, as if the nighttime vault were of metal, and not the planes that were crossing it, whose invisible trajectories ended in clusters of explosions more or less distant. The name given the infant was, however, suggested by destiny—which is to say, by events that took place that night in Sicily and in Italy; the name was even laden with destiny. Had he been born twelve

3

hours earlier in the city, which until then had never been bombarded, his name would have been Bruno: the name of Mussolini's son, who had died an aviator's death and who lived on in the hearts of all Italians such as the lawyer Munafò and his wife, Maria Grazia Munafò, née Cressi, daughter of Arturo Cressi, General of the Fascist Militia, hero of the wars in Ethiopia and in Spain but, because of subsequent rheumatism, somewhat less of a hero in the war then in progress. For the son born after the first and fearful bombardment of the city in which they resided, the parents chose instead the name Candido; the name had come spontaneously, almost surreally, to the father, and had been accepted by Signora Maria Grazia for the not entirely noble reason that it was so unlike the first choice of Bruno as virtually to erase the earlier intention. The name Candido was like a blank page on which, Fascism having been erased, a new life must be written. The existence of a book which bore that name as its title or of a character who meandered about in the wars between Abares and Bulgarians, between Jesuits and the Kingdom of Spain, was utterly unknown to the lawyer Francesco Maria Munafò, let alone the existence of François Marie Arouet, who had created the character. Unknown also to the Signora, who did read a book now and then, unlike her husband, who had never read one except for reasons of school or profession. That both persons should have gone through high school, *liceo*, and university without ever hearing mention of Voltaire and of Candide is no cause for amazement; it still happens.

The name Candido had exploded in the mind of the lawyer Munafò shortly after the explosions of that first and dreadful bombardment of the city in which he lived had stopped. He was near the railway station when, toward four o'clock in the afternoon, it had abruptly begun. He was almost running in order not to miss the train for Palermo, where, the next day, in that city's Court of Assizes he had to prove the innocence of a murderer. And all of a sudden it was as if he were inside a corolla the petals of which were formed by tremendous, almost precisely concentric explosions. He threw himself or he was thrown on the ground, his briefcase with the trial papers held close to his chest. After ten minutes—for, as he learned later, that was how long the bombardment had lasted—he got to his feet amid a stunned, terrified silence: a silence that was raining dust, dense, endless dust. But at first he was as if blind: it was his weeping, his tears, that opened his eyes to that rain of dust. When, centuries later, the dust began to clear, he saw that the street was no longer there, that the railway station was no longer there, that the city was no longer there. He emerged from the corolla by sliding down into the huge ditch that surrounded it and then laboriously climbing up the other side. And he found himself facing a grotesque plaster statue, in which only the eyes—as if just now transplanted, atrociously torn from a living man and transplanted in the statue—were alive. He spent some moments on the frontiers of madness before the briefcase he was still clutching to his chest cued him and he recognized himself—reflected in a mirror that had rained down almost intact from one of the houses that were now no longer there. He found himself uttering, repeating and repeating, the word "candid." Consciousness of who he was, of where he was, of what had happened jelled by virtue of that word. Candid/white, candid/pure—he felt encrusted in whiteness, and a sense of being reborn gushed within him. And still repeating the word, he was roused from that stunned and stupefied contemplation of himself in the dusty mirror by sudden anxiety, as painful as a wound he had not been aware of before, about what could have happened to his wife, to the child that was to be born any day, and to his home.

5

But he no longer knew in which direction his home lay: moving with a gait conceivably like that of a plaster statue, he went now this way, now that. Around him, groans began to be audible, and cries for help.

He wandered about, not knowing which direction to follow, until a patrol of soldiers, led by a very young officer, appeared among the ruins. Finding themselves face to face with that plaster statue, the soldiers laughed nervously. The officer asked him where he was going, what he was looking for. The lawyer gave the name of the street where he lived and his own name; the officer pulled a map of the city from his shoulder bag, oriented it by the smoking remains of the railway station, indicated the direction the lawyer should take to find his home, and expressed the hope that he might find it. "Thank you," the lawyer said, and he walked away through the rubble.

After several hours he found his house. Intact, except that all the doors and casement windows were open and almost torn off. Huddled in a corner, his wife and the maid, still in great agitation, were praying. The lawyer said a few prayers himself. Then they packed two suitcases with some bed linens and towels, collected jewelry, money, and bankbooks, and descended into the swollen human stream that was flowing toward the countryside.

They were instantly lucky. On the outskirts of town, a column of Army trucks had drawn up beneath the shelter of some trees. The entire fleeing mass clambered furiously into the trucks; when the captain ordered the soldiers to make them climb back down he was threatened, especially by the women, with having his eyes gouged out, with being chopped up for meatballs. The captain considered the situation: his soldiers were few, the enraged women were many. He gave orders to move. "Where to?" the soldiers asked. "Wherever

6

the road leads," the women replied in a chorus. Given the circumstances, it seemed a sensible answer. The trucks set out. They had traveled some twenty kilometers when those terrible twin-tailed American planes appeared. They gleamed in the evening light and it would have been fine to watch them descending as if they meant to land. Except that they opened up with machine guns. From the trucks, which had halted, the flight swarmed, howling with terror, into the open country.

When the machine guns had finished and the planes disappeared, all the trucks were in flames. There were three or four dead, about whom no one bothered. In that countryside, four hours after the strafing, in the grotto his parents presently discovered, Candido Munafò was born.

*About how the lawyer Munafò began to doubt
that he was the father of Candido, and about
the troubles that ensued from this*

After bringing Candido into the world before a hundred or
more women who were making a great to-do in that grotto
(a colleague of the lawyer Munafò who was present among
the refugees was reminded of the Norman Costanza, who in
the Piazza di Jesi, under a tent and surrounded by as many
women, brought the Emperor Frederick into this world),
Signora Maria Grazia Munafò née Cressi became, in the
judgment of her husband, a *different person*. In the judgment
of their men friends, more beautiful. Of their women friends
—and their judgment came closer to the husband's—more
severe in feature and feeling, more irritable and more irritating,
more venomous in speech, and more wandering in attention.
So that even before Christmas, the Signora found that she
had more men than women friends: this the lawyer Munafò
quite visibly found a cause for unease, for ill humor.

But although the Signora felt like a *different person* in her
body, which was as deliciously abuzz with appetites as a lively
amber-scented and sweetly dripping honeycomb, never for
one moment did it pass through her mind that from among
those men friends she could choose one for a furtive love
affair, which so many of her women friends, or ex-friends,
permitted themselves. Men interested her more than women
for one very simple reason: men engaged in politics, and at
that moment men who engaged in politics were something

8

she needed. General Arturo Cressi, her father, had from the very night on which Candido was born thought of himself, and wished to be thought of, as dead. Dead of fear, and on account of fear. But his daughter, who adored him, maintained that he felt dead and wished to be considered so because his native land was dead, Fascism was dead, and Mussolini had ended up a prisoner in German hands. She busied herself, therefore, in seeing—as she used to put it—that some glimmer of life was restored to the parental eye (indeed, her father had but one; the other he had lost in some, no one knew quite what, heroic action), which fear—but she believed the General's disillusion and disdain—had dimmed. And she chose the right path, the very path the General would have chosen had he been less afraid.

The General's most immediate fear was that the Americans would deport him to North Africa, as they were doing with all persons who were pointed out to them as dangerous Fascists. Maria Grazia quickly found a way of making this possible development impossible. Thanks, it must be said, to Candido. It was the first and only time that Candido was useful to the family for something. Since his mother had decided not to breast-feed him, unlike almost all mothers in that period, she first tried to give him asses' milk, which was considered very light and delicious by everyone who had never drunk it. Candido refused it. She then tried with diluted goats' milk, but to make him swallow that was a chore, nor, once it was swallowed, could he be prevented from throwing it up. In the countryside cows were no more. Lawyer Munafò was therefore obliged to abandon the patriotic dignity he had resolved to maintain toward the victorious enemy: he went to see the American captain who was in command of everything and everyone in the city; he put before him the famished state in which Candido was struggling to survive, and his yelping, especially at night, as well as the dilemma of Signora Maria Grazia and himself, the anguished and sleepless parents. The Captain was moved; he had powdered milk, condensed milk, evaporated milk, sugar, coffee, oatmeal, graham crackers, and canned meat sent to the house. Manna from Heaven, even for a house with a larder as well supplied as was that of Munafò.

The lawyer returned to thank the Captain. And this time, perhaps because the Captain had less to do, he talked with the lawyer more personally. He became the professor that he used to be—of Italian literature in a university—and not the captain with almost absolute and at times capricious powers which he appeared to be to everyone in the city. He spoke of his mother, and he showed the lawyer a color photo of her. His mother was Sicilian; from a village nearby, only fifteen kilometers away. But his mother did not remember having relatives in that village. From the last name, the lawyer tried to find some relatives for him; he knew the village well. And so they chatted pleasantly for several hours. When he got home, by way of an epigraph to his account of his conversation with the Captain, the lawyer enunciated to his wife the profound truth that had been revealed to him in the course of that conversation. "It's a small world," he said. The soldiers who at that moment were dying thousands of kilometers from their native land surely did not share this opinion, but Signora Munafò promptly concurred. She wished ultimately to make the world even smaller by inviting Captain John H. Dykes to dinner. The $\mathcal{H}$ stood for Hamlet, a revelation that so enchanted Maria Grazia that when they had reached a point of sufficient familiarity, she ended up calling the Captain simply "Hamlet." This pleased the Captain greatly, for, he said, that was what his mother used to call him.

Even before Captain John H. Dykes became Hamlet in the

Munafò household, the General had come to life again. To be precise: when the Captain went to dine at his daughter's home a second time. The third time, the General was there also. The General's Fascist past was not concealed from the Captain; actually, it impressed him favorably. His mother had always told him that thanks to Fascism Italians abroad had won a little respect.

The nightmare of deportation thus dispelled, Maria Grazia set about getting her father into politics, which, the prohibition of the Americans notwithstanding, were beginning to stir again. The General rather fancied the Communists, recalling a maxim that once, around 1930, Mussolini had confided to him. "Dear Arturo," the Duce had said to him (and in repeating the maxim, the General invested that "dear Arturo" with unbounded familiarity), "dear Arturo, if Fascism falls, only Communism will be left." Furthermore, among the frequent callers at the Munafò home was Paolo di Sales, lawyer and baron, who had been the General's aide-de-camp during the war in Spain (about which war he had written a book, *The Flower of Carmen and the Lictorian Fasces*), and who now, people said, might well be, *in pectore,* the local secretary of the Communist Party. But with Hamlet in the house, Maria Grazia would not allow any soft spot for the Communist Party. Either the Christian Democrats or the Liberals. It was fitting and proper that the General choose between those two parties. The General subdued his repugnance for priests by recalling that in Spain he had fought for the faith of Christ, and he chose the Christian Democrats.

Meantime, while Maria Grazia was building her father's fresh political fortunes, thanks to the milk and other prodigious American foodstuffs Candido was becoming quite different from the swarthy baby he had been in the first days of his life: he was growing both rosy and blond. More and more

11

he resembled John H. Dykes—Hamlet (whom the lawyer Munafò, with churlish stubbornness, continued to call "Jawn"). This ever more evident resemblance and the intimacy, the afflatus, that had grown up between Maria Grazia and Hamlet disturbed the lawyer Munafò to the point that there began darkly to form within him, like a tumor, a thought that could not be called thought, a suspicion that could not be called suspicion, a feeling that could not be called feeling. In moments when he came near to deciphering it, he laughed at himself, he mocked himself, he told himself he was mad. But there the tumor was, and it was growing. And it was this: that John H. Dykes might be the father of Candido; or that, in any event, he, Francesco Maria Munafò, might not be the father of Candido. It was pure madness: not only because at the moment Candido was conceived, Professor John H. Dykes was at Helena College, in Helena, Montana, but also, and above all, because Maria Grazia had never made love (in a manner of speaking, as we shall see later) with a man other than her lawyer husband.

This tumor spawned continual quarrels, which the lawyer, not wishing to confess the obscure reason for them even to himself, would incite on the most petty pretexts. And although appearances were always saved—in front of Hamlet, other friends, and the General—peace no longer prevailed in the Munafò household. Maria Grazia called her husband a "bumpkin" and a "mafioso," alluding to his not remote rustic origins and to his not precisely crystalline profession; the lawyer responded by calling her a "flirt," and each time it cost him a mental effort, a spasmodic control of his nerves, to have to substitute the word "flirt" for the word "whore," which sprang to his lips.

About the departure and the return of Hamlet,
and about what befell the lawyer Munafò
deservedly and Candido undeservedly

John H. Dykes left immediately after the Christmas holidays, which in the Munafò home were, what with the contribution of American military victualing, notably abundant in food and drink.

After Hamlet's departure the lawyer regained relative peace of mind. Only it upset him to look at Candido, who more and more resembled Hamlet; and once when Maria Grazia, in utter innocence, at a moment when she wanted peace and not war with her husband, said, "But do you notice how much he looks like Hamlet?," the lawyer felt the wing of madness lift him up and make him, in turn, lift and violently pull toward himself a corner of the tablecloth on which plates, glasses, and cutlery had been set out for dinner. His sudden, furious movement, the noise, the crockery, wine, and sauces crashing to the floor made Maria Grazia mute with terror for a moment. Then came a torrent of words and tears. The lawyer, who neither could nor would explain the reason for his action, and who on the other hand felt obscurely in the right for having done what he had done, and therefore in the right not to excuse himself, escaped for two days to the country. Upon his return, his wife was armored in silence. The behavior of the maid, ever the Signora's faithful ally, was, on the contrary, wrathful and rude.

Maria Grazia's impenetrable silence was accounted for by

13

the fact that she had made a decision: to leave a man whom she now realized she had never loved—and with cause, she told herself; what's more, a man who seemed to her prey to a madness that he had heretofore managed to conceal but now enjoyed giving vent to with no restraint whatever. He was torturing her. And he was enjoying it.

Maria Grazia was twenty-four years old; she had a great longing to be loved, to love, to have a good time, to see the world. She questioned herself about her love for Candido. All that much love she did not find, despite his resemblance to Hamlet. If she were to leave the child, not one of her friends or acquaintances would forgive her, but she found sufficient reason for forgiving herself. The trauma, for her, of the day Candido was born, of how he was born, worked obscurely to make her renunciation no cause for drama, their separation no cause for pain. Rather, it was the General who had to be thought about: her abandoning what the law termed "the conjugal roof" must not harm the success with which the General appeared to be launched in the Catholics' party. Things must be done properly: judicious use must be made of the Catholics' party, the priests, the Church. Even had there been divorce in Italy at the time, Maria Grazia would have preferred to free herself of her husband through the Sacred Roman Rota, however long and humiliating the proceedings. Humiliating because of everything, whether lie or truth, that she would have to say, and would have to have said, about her own body. And in her case the line to be taken—chosen by lawyers who were specialized and priests who were consummately versed in the matter—would be that she, no sooner touched by her husband, would grow rigid and then faint, so that her husband gave vent to his desire on what might as well have been a dead woman, if indeed upon his first approaches he himself were not unmanned and

14

so lost heart. Which was beginning to become quite true—objective proof of the insane despair that had insinuated itself into his being and that now, no longer an abstraction but a fact, was growing and blinding him with rage. The lawyer now spent almost all his time in the country; Maria Grazia was therefore freer, and between lawyers and prelates, and always accompanied by the General, was weaving the procedures for annulling the marriage.

During the lawyer's absence, Hamlet returned on a two-week leave. He arrived like a husband, like a real husband, like the real husband. Although there had never been a contact between them that went further than a handshake (their farewell handshake longer and more throbbing) or an understanding that went beyond tenderly laughing or wistfully confiding glances, when Hamlet set foot again in the Munafò home, they embraced; they kissed each other on the cheek, and then, after a moment of luminous hesitation, long on the mouth. As in a film, Maria Grazia thought later, as in an American film. And everything happened so simply, so naturally, that to undress, to go to bed, to make love was in the order of things, in the order of life, of being alive. And so, for the first time, Maria Grazia knew love. To the great joy of the maid also, even if hers was different from that of the Signora; for the maid—Concetta by name—joy consisted principally in the fact that finally, factually, she could, at least mentally, call the lawyer Munafò a cuckold.

In the adjoining room, Candido's eyes were following the flight of the cupids and roses painted on the ceiling. That ceiling was his universe. He was a very quiet baby.

About the solitude of the lawyer Munafò,
and about that of Candido

The proceedings for the annulment of the marriage, as had been foreseen, were long. The outcome was certain; that is, the annulment would surely be granted, but the time to weigh so difficult and delicate a matter must necessarily be long. Lawyer Munafò was not contesting the action. It was very true that Maria Grazia had never loved him (loved him so little—but this he thought without saying it—as to have brought a son into the world who resembled the man she would later meet and love); it was very true that she grew rigid under his caresses, that her eyes became glazed, that she lost consciousness. So the suit inched along its inevitable length.

Meanwhile, Maria Grazia had moved, first into her father's house, then to another city, where, it was said, she was living in a *pensione* or in a convent. In fact, depending on where Hamlet was transferred, she was moving from one city to another, but secretly, so as not to compromise the outcome of the suit and out of respect for the man who, in the eyes of the law, was still her husband. Respect that was also due him for the way in which, in relation to the Sacred Roman Rota, he was conducting himself: correctly, loyally. By this time, he, too, could not wait to be freed of that marriage bond, even though he had no intention of remarrying and had, indeed, become something of a misogynist. Solitude beckoned to him smilingly, a solitude that would be sealed by a sentence not

16

only pronounced by an ecclesiastical court but also "scrutinized by a foreign power"—a phrase he had always professionally relished now held for him the savor of freedom—which is to say, by a court of the Italian state. There was just one complication, and that came from Candido. Both people, husband and wife, found themselves bound to a terrible pretense and were found to be so by the society in which they lived, by relatives, friends, priests, and lawyers. They had to pretend, each contending against the other, to want Candido and to be unwilling to surrender him, whether she to him, or he to her.

Had there been a King Solomon to decide whether Candido should be entrusted to his father or to his mother, perhaps the poor child would have been divided in two, such was the obstinacy that father and mother exhibited in wanting him. Luckily for Candido, when the moment of decision came, in November, 1945, there were involved a genial judge of the Kingdom of Italy, lawyers, priests, and a chorus of relatives and friends. And furthermore, this decision which was so difficult to make had in fact already been made the instant Maria Grazia set the procedural wheels in motion: Candido must remain with his father; the principal reason was—everyone recognized it as a reason, even the women—that a woman who dared be unresigned to staying until her death with a husband she did not love and who did not love her had a just measure of punishment coming to her. And what better punishment than this: to deprive her of her son forever? That, in actual fact, the situation was altogether different—that it would be a punishment for the husband to keep Candido with him, and one more freedom for Maria Grazia not to have him—was unimportant: what was important was to confirm a rule and to maintain appearances. With due respect for rule and appearances, the lawyer Munafò appeared to be vindictively pleased, vindictively happy to have won the match to keep Candido himself, while Maria Grazia appeared dolorous in defeat. However, the person truly defeated was the lawyer: he was forced to keep the son he did not love, the son he could not feel was his son, and whom, unspeakably, in his secret rage, he did not call "Candido" but "the American."

Ever more rosy, ever more blond, serene, and smiling, Candido did not feel the slightest prick from the bed of thorns in which he was living. He seemed able to make out happily without a mother and a father. For his most vital and immediate needs, he was not able to do without Concetta, who was committed to maternal love for him and scorn for the lawyer; but not even toward Concetta did he demonstrate an attachment that went beyond the business of eating, drinking, and other needs, and the pleasure of a game of where-is-Candido, which Concetta would sometimes play with him. A game, it must be said, that entertained Candido for ten minutes at most, after which he lost interest and returned to his solitary, private play. His games—we can try to define them only approximately—were like crossword puzzles which he could play with things. Adults make words cross, but Candido made things cross. Words did come into the game also, almost always just the first or the last syllable; but primarily the game was based on things, the place of things, the uses they were put to, their shape, color, weight, and consistency, which made it agreeably difficult, agreeably chancy, as a game should be.

The supreme eulogy Concetta used to make of Candido was this: "He's a baby who stays where you put him." He knew how to get along with other babies provided they were not rough, and he knew how to be alone; he would stay quiet for hours wherever Concetta left him. He had an innate but—if one can say this of an infant—a formal politeness. He was sufficient unto himself: that was the whole of it. According to Concetta—who was herself very nervous—he was a child who had no nerves. "You would never believe," she used to say, "that he was born on that night in hell." But she also thought that that night in hell had caused him to be born if not exactly stupid, then a bit slow, a bit dull-witted. And when she thought this, she loved him even more, and would call him "my joy," "my baby Jesus," "my own." Candido responded to these effusions with a polite smile that became tolerant when Concetta would smother him with furious kisses. He did not like to be smothered with kisses, but he tolerated it. He tolerated also the kisses of the General, his grandfather, although they bothered him a little because of the General's Vandyke beard—the one thing unchanged in the old hero of the Fascist wars, now become a Christian Democrat, a republican, and, of course, an anti-Fascist.

When all the political things he had to attend to left him time, the General would go see Candido, or he would have him fetched to his house by Concetta. Despite the sesame crackers and the raisins, which he liked, Candido was very bored in his grandfather's house. From the day, later on, when the General took a rifle from among the many he had hung on his walls, and, in the garden, showed him how it was loaded and fired, every time Concetta announced, "Now we're going to your grandfather the General's house," Candido would say, firmly, no; and if Concetta insisted, his eyes would fill with tears. That was enough to make her retreat. "No, joy of my life, we're not going. If you don't want to go, we aren't going." And she asked herself, "What has that wicked old man done to him?," for whatever revulsion Candido showed, however gratuitous or indecipherable, she took it unquestionably to be right and professed it herself.

19

Once, when the General remonstrated about Candido's visits having stopped, Concetta was obliged to tell him that the decision was Candido's, and was inflexible. "But why?" the General asked. "How should I know? *You* should know," Concetta replied. This reply sent the General into a rage, but when he had calmed down he recalled that the last time Candido had been brought to him, he had had him see and hear how a rifle is fired, and he pronounced upon Candido the scornful verdict: "He's chicken!"

*About how Candido arrived at the state of being
an almost total orphan; and about the risk
he ran of emigrating to Helena, Montana*

At five years of age, Candido knew almost everything about
the lawyer Munafò, and the lawyer knew nothing about
Candido, nor did it matter to him that he should know something. Food, cleanliness, and toys the boy did not lack for.
What more could be expected of a father who—although his
putative paternity was not supported by Holy Writ—resembled Joseph the son of Jacob, whose wife had conceived
through the power of the Holy Spirit, as had Maria Grazia
through the power of the American Spirit. There had never
been the slightest need to scold the child; if only there had
been, the lawyer thought grimly now and then. Not even a
need to urge, to prod him to eat; the boy always ate with
good appetite, and was even prudently greedy. Never had
there been occasion to forbid him some dangerous game.
Candido did not like dangerous games. As for insisting that
he sleep in the hours when he should sleep, never had it
happened that at the prescribed hours Candido refused and
protested; he would go to sleep as soon as his head touched
the pillow, "like an angel," as Concetta put it.

Candido, then, knew almost everything about his father;
which is to say, apart from his father's thoughts, he knew
everything that concerned his profession, his income from
that profession and from his farm properties, his relationships
with clients, colleagues, judges, tenants, and farm hands. He

knew this the way President Nixon's tapes knew everything that President Nixon said. Except that Nixon knew about the tapes, and the lawyer Munafò did not know about Candido's listening; this made a difference as to the consequences of the disaster both encountered, it being verifiable that Munafò was less of an imbecile than Nixon.

Candido had got into the habit of slipping into his father's office in the afternoon, at vespers, when the light, which was violent in every other part of the house, in that room with its dark, heavy furniture, dark leather armchairs, dark damask draperies, acquired a soft, steamy, sleepy-making quality. Candido used to settle down behind a large divan and, stretched out on the thick rug that covered almost the entire floor, he would tirelessly explore the paintings on the ceiling. Sometimes it would happen that, staring now at one, now at another of the nude women who flitted across it, he would feel sleep drifting down on him like one of the azure veils the women or the wind waved; in a word, it would happen that he fell deliciously asleep. The ceilings of rooms were his textbooks: he had promoted himself from cupids and roses to nude women and veils.

When he did fall asleep amid the lightness and sweetness of that veil lovingly surrendered to him by one of the ladies on the ceiling—almost always by the one who was his favorite —he would awaken the moment his father came in, threw open the windows, and sat down at his desk. However, Candido would lie motionless and silent, waiting for the visitors to begin arriving. If he grew bored, he would slip silently on his belly, shielded by the furniture from his father's view, and pass through one of the three doors in the office by which no one entered or left, hidden like the others by heavy draperies. But it rarely happened that he did become bored: he took pleasure in that kind of invisible theater, the dialogue, the varying volume and timbre of the voices, the dramatic or imploring or persuasive tone that they assumed, the Sicilian speech of the peasants, his father's Italian. There was not a shred of mischievousness, of course, in that hiding and listening: his remaining there silently and his slithering away were simply tricks in a game he was playing by himself.

This game, aesthetic or, on a slightly lower level, sensual in nature, rarely quickened Candido's interest in the facts that were being set forth; first, the facts were poorly, incoherently set forth; and even when very clearly set forth by the protagonists or by their relatives, or when clearly synthesized by his father, the facts almost always remained very obscure to Candido. This was lucky for the lawyer Munafò and for his clients. But it was luck that could not last; and, in fact, last it did not.

One afternoon, Candido found himself listening to the confession of a murder. He had heard Concetta talk about that murder with loathing, with horror. Later, he had heard his companions at nursery school talk about it, especially the son of the lieutenant in the Carabinieri, who was mighty proud of the fact that his father had arrested the murderer. In his father's office that afternoon, Candido learned instead that the lieutenant had not arrested the killer but a man who had, yes, his reasons for murdering the murderee, but even though masked, though secret, his reasons were not so serious as those of the person who really had killed him. Candido had no exact notion about killing, or dying, or death. Or, rather, he had the same notion as Concetta: dying was a kind of trip; it was leaving one place to go to another. The confession the man made to his father, in order to get advice about how he should behave in the event that the innocence of the innocent man were to be recognized and that the suspicions of

23

the Carabinieri were to fall upon him, made an impression on Candido as he imagined the impression such a revelation would have made upon the son of the lieutenant. Therefore, he made careful mental notes of the conversation, including the name of the assassin. And punctually, the next day, he detailed the facts to his nursery-school companions, by way of telling the lieutenant's son that his father had made a mistake. Whereupon, no less punctually, the lieutenant's son reproached his father for making him cut a poor figure with his companions by arresting innocent people instead of guilty people.

Pandemonium ensued. The Carabinieri arrived in force at the nursery school; in the presence of the headmistress and several teachers, they had Candido relate everything; and everything that Candido had heard in his father's office he related meticulously and with pleasure at finding himself among so many Carabinieri, who with pleasure were listening to him.

When he left the nursery school, he found Concetta waiting for him as usual, only she was uglier than usual for the tears she had been shedding and now with difficulty held back. She told him that his father had gone away, had gone on a very long trip. The news would have been received by Candido with his customary indifference—his father was always leaving for the country, for Palermo, for Rome—if Concetta had not had that tearful face and if she had not added a phrase that to Candido seemed both meaningless and alarming. "I," Concetta said, "should cut your tongue out."

Later he was able to learn, but confusedly, some details about his father's departure. It seemed (he never knew this precisely, and indeed did not want to) that, the Carabinieri having departed, the headmistress of the nursery school had made haste to inform the lawyer Munafò of what Candido had related to the Carabinieri; and the lawyer, feeling he had

24

failed both his profession and the rules by which, as a man, he had lived until that moment, had put an end to his life. In going on this trip, he attempted to restore the rules that Candido had unknowingly infringed upon: he wrote that he was taking his own life because he was weary, because he was ill, with cancer perhaps, nerves perhaps. A noble lie, which did not, however, spare the client whose confession Candido had related a sentence of twenty-seven years in prison.

Meanwhile, that same day Concetta took Candido to the home of the General. The little boy remained there until his mother's arrival—an arrival that signaled for Candido the onset of an entire month of tribulations, for his mother came believing it was her duty to have her son live with her and to carry him off to Helena, Montana, where she was now living as Mrs. John H. Dykes.

This woman—his mother, that is—Candido found pleasing. She seemed to him to resemble his favorite among the nudes on the ceiling. And it would have pleased him (Stendhal!) if when she picked him up in her arms and hugged him there had been no clothes between her and him. But as for going to America with her, that was quite another matter. He wanted to stay with Concetta, and in the house with the beautiful painted ceilings. His tears and, presently, a desperate flight (they found him ragged and famished, wandering about the countryside) convinced his mother to leave him. A decision, it must be said, that was a relief for her, too. But when Candido returned her kisses coldly as she was leaving him, she whispered to her father, "He's a little monster." A thought that the General was already nursing on his own.

*About the compassionate censure of which Candido
was the object on the part of the General, relatives,
and virtually the entire city, and about his behavior
when he became aware of it*

A month before the lawyer Munafò committed suicide, the
General had been elected to Parliament, winning so many
preferential votes on the Christian Democratic ticket that he
outran every other candidate elected in western Sicily. At the
outset of the electoral campaign, his opponents had tried to
attack him for his Fascist warrior's past, but in the crowds
listening at these meetings the attacks produced a measure
of admiration for the General; and then the General had
threatened to counterattack by listing the names, posts, and
perquisites of Fascist candidates on the slates of other parties,
and there were many such. The local candidate of the Communist Party was Baron Paolo di Sales, who, as we have said,
had served as aide-de-camp to the General during the war in
Spain, and who now was his closest opponent in the campaign.
But both men conducted themselves with a discretion and
delicacy that went so far as reciprocal affirmations of respect
and esteem: and this, publicly. And the Baron was elected
also.

At the last public meeting the General held, Concetta, who
was a fanatical propagandist more for the party of the Cross
of Christ than for the General, who belonged to that party,
wanted Candido to be present, too. Candido was bored and
disgusted: too many people, too many voices, too many

26

drunken breaths; and he smelled those breaths the more be-cause so many people felt duty-bound to bend over him, pat his head, and ask him wasn't he glad that the General, his grandfather, might become a deputy. Candido did not know what a deputy was, and anyhow he cared not a rap whether his grandfather became a deputy or not.

Once elected—a personal triumph in the victory the party of Christian Democracy won on April 18, 1948—the General seemed rejuvenated. Already during the electoral campaign he had started to wear a black patch over his missing eye; now that he was so rejuvenated by his electoral success, the patch gave him a piratical, predatory air that worked like a charm on the Ladies of the Sacred Heart, the Ursulines, and the Daughters of Mary. In his renewed self-assurance and boldness, when the General spoke of his ex-son-in-law (doubly ex, because of the Sacred Roman Rota and because of death), he would say, "He was an idiot. If he had come immediately to me, I would have fixed everything." And if he happened to say this when Candido was present, he glanced down at him with mingled scorn and commiseration.

All of Candido's other relatives looked upon him with the same sentiments—those on his father's side stinting on the commiseration—as did men who had been friends of his father and women who had been friends of his mother. Only Concetta, after that comment had slipped out about how she ought to cut out his tongue, looked upon him without a shadow of censure but with abundant, tearful pity. And, in all truth, Concetta's unqualified pity caused Candido more an-noyance than did the ambiguous sentiments of the others. In a word, all of them caused him annoyance and disgust, some more and some less, but Concetta most of all. He therefore set about observing her, studying her. He became aware that Concetta had radically changed her feelings with regard to the defunct lawyer and that her new feelings, amounting almost to a cult, were combined with remorse for her erstwhile bitterness and derision. At the same time, her feelings with regard to Signora Maria Grazia had also changed. Candido could neither know nor divine this, but the insult "cuckold," which Concetta had so often lavished mentally on the lawyer, had now been changed to "whore," and was lavished with the same frequency on the absent Signora Maria Grazia. Lawyer Munafò came to thank her for this change in feeling, appearing to her in a dream; and he seized the occasion to ask that she have some Masses sung for him, since, he said, there where he was, they regarded him as forgotten and treated him accordingly.

Concetta told Candido about the request and was silent about the thanks. She also shared with him her deduction and conviction that the lawyer was in Purgatory, for if someone is in Hell, what good can Masses do him? And from that moment on, there was a shower of Masses to refrigerate the spot in Purgatory where the lawyer found himself; at each of them, in a church draped in black, were present Concetta, compunctiously and frantically praying, and Candido, his prayers offered less compunctiously, indeed with boredom and inattention. It was during one of these Masses that, what with one thought leading to another, Candido discovered that death is terrible not because one is no longer here but, on the contrary, because one is here still, at the mercy of the fickle memories, fickle feelings, fickle thoughts of those who remain behind: like his father in the memories, feelings, and thoughts of Concetta. What drudgery it must be for the dead person to wander about still in what the living remembered, felt, and thought; even in what they dreamed. In Candido's imagination, it was like a brutal recall, a whistle that signaled the start of a race, a gasping, broken-winded arrival. What Concetta called "the other life" was literally a dog's life.

For his part, Candido disturbed his father very little in his "other life" (which, to tell the truth, the boy considered rather improbable), and only insofar as remembering him was useful in understanding why people looked at him with both censure and pity. He came quickly to an explanation for the pity. Or better: he believed he had found an explanation when he noticed at school that another little boy who had lost his parents and who lived with his grandparents was treated in the same fashion. In fact, but this he became aware of only later, the pity people visited on him was different; it was complicated by a preoccupation about what would happen to him inside when he learned, as sooner or later he would, that his father died because he had said a thing he should not have said. As for the censure, this required a more prolonged and arduous interrogation. Observing Concetta, and sometimes provoking her; storing away in his memory and mulling over everything that his grandfather, relatives, and acquaintances said about his father; summing up again and again his memories of afternoons spent in his father's office, stretched out on the rug and hidden by the divan; juxtaposing each element as if it were part of the handsome wood puzzle he had been given, the single pieces of which he loved to see, touch, and smell more than the constructions that could be fashioned with them, Candido arrived at an image that was not yet a judgment nor was it as clear as we are presenting it now: the image of his father as that of a man who adds up his whole life and arrives at a sum indicating that it would be right for him to put a bullet through his head. This image had innocently crystallized for him from the many deals he had seen his father make; but the General, Concetta, and all the others would have thought it born of the most unthinkable and monstrous cynicism.

Although Concetta knew nothing of this image, Candido began to seem a monster to her when he was about ten, as he had seemed to his mother and his grandfather when he was five. From Concetta's point of view, he was a monster to whom one owed more love than if he had been "like other children." Candido had no cult for his dead father, he did not ask for news of his living mother, he was not fond of his grandfather, and he cared not a fig for her. What's more, he would say things that made her shiver, and he said them in a way that had something diabolic about it: laughing shrilly and fitting his words to music. Thus, once he told her, "You don't want to say it to me in so many words, but I know I killed my father." And he whirled off, exactly like a devil; for, according to Concetta, like colts, devils were always running, and they spoke to music, and their laughter was like a honing of knives.

*About the concern of the General and of Concetta
for Candido's education, and about the General's
decision to give him, as in bygone days, a tutor*

Several times Concetta resolved to speak with the General about Candido's manifesting signs of diabolism, but each time she put it off with the excuse either that she found the General busy, that he seemed to her incapable of understanding, or that one should wait another week or so to see whether Candido might mend. In fact, Concetta feared that the General would decide to send Candido to boarding school. Devil or not, what would her life be without Candido?

Instead of going to the General, she went to talk to the Archpriest. And the Archpriest, Concetta's recommendations notwithstanding, spoke to the General, but not in the terms, naturally, in which Concetta had spoken to him. The tale of the diabolic spirit that had insinuated itself in the boy made him laugh, on the one hand, and, on the other, it worried him. Which is to say, it worried him that the boy should be living with a woman as ignorant, superstitious, and full of superstitious terrors as Concetta. Perhaps what appeared diabolic to Concetta was nothing other than Candido's healthy defense, his healthy rebellion against her funereal religious zeal, her continual, meticulous cult of the dead and of death, her obscure beliefs and penances.

The Archpriest was considered, and considered himself, "modern." He applied himself diligently to the study of psychology, concealing in this word, however, the other term

31

which in those days in Italy was to be pronounced with caution and many reservations: psychoanalysis. In fact, he had written an essay, "Moral Psychology," which is to say, psychoanalysis; the tidy manuscript lay, as if lodged among rocks, in the bishop's palace, awaiting the imprimatur. The rocks were the bishop's indecision whether to grant or withhold permission, and he was more of a mind to withhold it, for not only had he perceived behind the word "psychology" the word "psychoanalysis" but also he found excessive and revolutionary the subtly defended theory that the Church should recognize and take up psychology, which is to say, psychoanalysis, as a substantive, almost connatural, and irrenunciable element of its ministry, of ecclesiastical service; it should not be left in lay hands. And the way not to leave it in lay hands was through a kind of spiritual "coup": the status of deacon should be bestowed on all those in the Catholic world who, willingly or not, practice the profession of psychology—which is to say, of psychoanalysis. For that matter, theologically speaking, the figure of deacon had such uncertain, such undefined outlines . . .

Given these inclinations and these studies, one can readily infer how much the case of Candido, as Concetta had outlined it, would arouse the interest of Archpriest Lepanto. Accordingly, he spoke to the General about it, and the General confessed to him that he, too, was concerned about how the child was growing up, about the strange ideas he had. The Archpriest offered to occupy himself with the matter: they should send the boy to him ostensibly for private tutoring; he would help him in his lessons but at the same time he would be observing, studying, analyzing him.

Candido began willingly to frequent the Archpriest. It amused him greatly to discover little by little, in one conversation after another, what a priest was like: this mysterious man, sheathed in his long black gown, who by donning silk damasks and laces, behold, made the wafer become the body of Christ and obtained a dead man's passage from Purgatory to Paradise (powers that, according to Concetta, it was a sacrilege to doubt but that Candido doubted). The Archpriest, sheathed in the diving suit of his schemata and cabala, felt like a deep-sea diver spying upon, and surprising, and penetrating Candido's thoughts and mental images which might, it was to be hoped, serve in some measure to confirm those schemata and that cabala. Actually, it was Candido who was spying on and analyzing the Archpriest.

Physically, there was something catlike about Candido: something soft, velvety, indolent; a drowsy, absent gaze that at moments narrowed and quickened with attention; slow, silent movements that at times became soundlessly brisk. His mind was the same: full of fantasies, volatile and whimsical, but always alert. Besides, it pleased him to resemble a cat: to be free, as he knew he was; to have no ties to the people around him; to be sufficient unto himself. Actually, the one bond he felt he had was, indeed, with the house cat: a handsome gray cat who was just his age and therefore, being a cat, the age of his grandfather. The moment Candido learned how to measure out a cat's life, he called the cat "Grandfather." This, when the General accidentally heard of it, he took in sufficiently ill part to write it to his daughter. "He calls the cat 'Grandfather,'" he wrote. And his daughter answered facetiously: "I told you, he's a little monster."

Up to a point, the Archpriest also was convinced that he was a little monster. As they analyzed each other, the Archpriest had discovered nothing that was valid for a diagnosis and for consequent therapy, whereas Candido had discovered that the Archpriest had a kind of fixed idea, rather complicated but reducible, more or less, to these terms: all little boys kill their fathers, and some of them, sometimes, kill even Our Father Who is in Heaven. Except that it is not really killing; it is like a game in which names take the place of things and instead of actions there are intentions; in a word, a game like the Mass. That the Archpriest should think this of all little boys chagrined Candido more for the sake of the Archpriest than for the sake of little boys. That he should think this of him made Candido decide that it behooved him, with all due patience, to disabuse the Archpriest. In every way, he gave him to understand, and at times told him clearly, that, yes, it could be that all little boys kill their fathers and Our Father Who is in Heaven, but that he, Candido, most certainly had not: he had not killed his father, and he knew nothing, nor did he want to know anything, about that other Father.

Candido's attitude perturbed the Archpriest, and caused him a crisis of conscience. Because, according to the Archpriest, Candido had indeed killed his father; therefore, one had either to convince him that he had killed his father or to leave him in his arrogant innocence. A dreadful dilemma, on the order of the one in which a fellow in an American short story found himself: he wishes to verify a version of the theory of probabilities as set forth in the example of the twelve chimpanzees that tap at random on twelve type-writers and ultimately write all the works in the Library of Congress. Accordingly, he buys twelve chimpanzees and twelve typewriters, and behold, immediately—not *ultimately* —the chimps reproduce Dante, Shakespeare, and Dickens. And so the man has no recourse but to kill all twelve. To be truly quit of his problem, the Archpriest would have had to kill Candido—an idea that, it must be said to his credit, did not occur to him. And so he remained saddled with the problem, unable to bring himself to resolve it. But, on the other hand, neither was Candido able to resolve his with regard to the Archpriest.

Thus, facing each other for years across a table on which stood a bronze crucifix, a pewter inkwell, the Acts of the Apostles, and the collected works of Freud and Jung, they scrutinized each other, spied on each other. They talked about many things, but always that idea of discovering each other was present to both. And thus they came to love each other, beyond any fathers and any Our Father in Heaven.

About the things of which Candido and the
Archpriest used to talk, and about the vexation
this caused the General

Candido got rid of his schoolwork with dispatch, by himself
and at home. The Archpriest rarely found any errors, and
when he did happen to find one, Candido's quickness in
recognizing and correcting it spared him having to explain. So,
the scholastic part speedily disposed of, they talked of other
things; which is to say, without the Archpriest's realizing
it, the things Candido wished them to talk about.

They talked about Concetta and the General; the Archpriest talked about himself, about his poverty-ridden child-
hood in a poverty-ridden world, about his mother, about
his father, about his adolescence and youth at the Theological
Seminary in the capital city of the province, about the day
he was ordained a priest, and about the celebration with which
this was hailed in his home village. They spoke of Concetta
and the General as of two themes that between them ex-
hausted everything in human life that was error, stupidity,
madness. Candido had a fantastic image of the two, as if
they were enwrapped and hidden by funereal climbing vines.
The image had come to him from the ivy that had covered
the ruins of the ancient church in the cemetery; he wanted
to see the ruins that were hidden in Concetta and in the
General. The Archpriest spoke willingly of Concetta, because
the many Catholics like Concetta were the cause of his
priestly anxieties, anxieties that at times were close to

desperation. He was loath, however, to speak of the General. Having ascertained that for Candido the General had not replaced his father, just as Concetta had not replaced his mother, he would have preferred to speak with the boy not of the General but of his faraway mother, now married to a man whom Candido did not know and the mother of two other sons, equally unknown to Candido. But for Candido, his mother, the man whom she had married, and his two American brothers were so remote that he rarely thought of them; and when he did happen to think of them, it was with a vague curiosity about their faraway and surely different life, but never with any feeling that resembled a sense of deprivation, envy, or mortification. It can be said flatly that he thought of them without any feeling whatever; and so true was this that when he began to learn to write and, at the General's suggestion, the Archpriest urged him to write a little letter to his mother, it was only out of civility toward the Archpriest that he did not say no. The letter began, "Dear Signora," and dryly advised that everyone was well: he, Concetta, the cat, the General, and the Archpriest. Reading it, at first the Archpriest almost lost his temper; then, in the light of his science, he contemplated the letter and rejoiced. "But what's this? You call your mama 'Dear Signora'?" Patiently, Candido rewrote it, with the sole variant of "Dear Mama." But the matter did not end there. The Archpriest's appetite had been whetted; it became hunger when Candido spoke to him about the nude woman on the ceiling; it seemed to him like a game, Candido said, like make-believe, as if he were writing to a woman who existed only in that painting. The Archpriest thought: There, to reject his mother, to punish her for having abandoned him, he has identified her with the nude woman on the ceiling. Because given the idea he has of a mama and of nudity, a mama cannot be nude. Therefore

37

he set about dissuading Candido from the identification on which he had become fixated, but Candido insisted so stubbornly that the image of his mother was there, flitting across the ceiling, that the Archpriest wanted to see it.

When he did, he was somewhat taken aback. The fact that the painted woman truly did so resemble Maria Grazia as to make one think she herself might have posed nude for the artist (an impossibility, since in one corner of the ceiling, under the artist's signature, was written the year 1904) sparked a certain agitation in the Archpriest in the zone—delicate, translucent, and carefully kept submerged—of the senses. Sounding out what Candido candidly said, he saw it could not be that the boy was moved by any dark wish to degrade his mother when he identified her with the nude woman. The contemplation of that body to which he used now and then to abandon himself was like a desire purified of every instinct, every feeling, even of desire itself: it was, literally, an idyl, a moment of accord with the world, a moment of harmony. The Archpriest noticed in himself, however, the surge of a strange and insane passion. He therefore decided not to talk with Candido about his mother any more, which was something of a relief for Candido, although at moments he was curious to understand why the Archpriest no longer spoke of her. His relief came, actually, from the fact that a painful subject was no longer touched on, the pain for him lying in the memory (and in the threat, which he felt ever hanging over his head) of his mother's coming to take him with her to America.

So they talked about Concetta and the General, and the Archpriest talked about himself, shrewdly urged on by Candido. Not that Candido knew he was being so shrewd: he merely felt, with no unfriendliness or sense of guilt, curious. He considered this curiosity similar to the kind one invested in learning the way one's school wished one to, learning facts about the past, about the climates and products of faraway lands, about the three kingdoms of nature (this division of nature into three kingdoms did not seem to him natural), or how to solve a problem in arithmetic. That was it: the people close to him were like problems, and he wanted to solve them and also to be quit of them, the way by solving the problems he was assigned in school, he got quit of them. And at a certain moment, the most important of these persons, these problems, became for him the General. That is to say, Fascism. And that is to say, the past along whose border line with the present he himself had been born.

This line, according to what was said on national holidays, especially on April 25th, which commemorated the liberation of all Italy from Fascism, had seemingly separated the shadows from the light, night from day, and since the General had been in the middle, it had accordingly cut him in half. The proof of this for Candido was that eye, the loss of which was concealed by the patch; it belonged to the half of his grandfather that had remained in the shadows. For Candido, the more immediate problem was this: Could a man thus cut in half live with all the energy and relish the General exhibited? For there was no doubt: one half of his grandfather continued to live (or to die, if Fascism was dead) in his past. All the relics he kept in his bedroom bespoke this: tiny triangular flags of watered silk, black on one side, tricolored on the other, and bordered with gold fringe; medals; inscribed photographs from Mussolini, Badoglio, Generalissimo Franco. (When the General said "el Generalissimo," Candido had the impression that on the first syllables he was crunching a liqueur-filled candy and on the last savoring the taste of it.)

When submitted to the Archpriest, the problem was given this solution: in his youth, the General had made a mistake;

he had continued to make a mistake for twenty years; but since the error had cost him great sacrifices, not the least of which was the loss of an eye—well, he cherished the receipts the homeland and Fascism had given him for those sacrifices. But when this indulgent solution was proposed to the General, it elicited a terrible outburst. "I made no mistake, I have never made a mistake!" he shouted, and he launched into a tirade about Fascism that we can summarize thus: Fascism had been great, whereas all Italians had been small and vile (except, of course, General Cressi and a few others). When he ran out of breath, Candido said tranquilly, "It was the Archpriest who told me you had made a mistake back then." Had he said this before, the General would have been more prudent, given the fact that so many of the votes that had sent him to Parliament came to him through the Archpriest. Now he could not eat his words. Flushed with mute anger, he strode up and down. Candido took advantage of the silence to ask placidly, "Did you make a mistake then, or are you making a mistake now?" The General halted before him and, visibly restraining himself from cuffing his ears, roared, "But what mistakes, worm that you are! It's the same thing!," and he went raging out of the room.

Candido was struck less by having been called a worm than by the mysterious statement "It's the same thing." What was the same thing? The past and the present? Fascism and anti-Fascism? He asked elucidation of the Archpriest, reporting to him word for word what his grandfather had said.

The Archpriest was much disturbed. He gave Candido no satisfaction, and said that he would speak with the General, but it was clear that he was angry, that he was seething.

He did, in fact, speak with the General. And it was a collision, to judge from the consequences that the colloquy had for Candido. The General not only continued to call him worm, crawling worm, filthy worm, but also tattletale, spy, informer, traitor to his relatives, spy and traitor from the day of his birth. Candido held his peace under that hailstorm. He was a bit concerned when the General threatened to stop the afterschool lessons with the Archpriest.

*About the power that Candido did not know he had
over his nearest of kin, and about his impressions
and his actions when he found out that he had it*

Candido was rich, thanks to what his father had left him, to which was added the dowry of his mother, who, in the agreements following on the annulment of her marriage, had passed it on to him by gracious deed of gift. Of this fortune, the General was legal guardian. The guardian of Candido, in legal parlance; guardian of both his affects and his effects. Nor would the General have dreamed of nibbling at his grandson's properties and rents; on the contrary, he was a scrupulous administrator. But he did derive from them, or he thought he derived from them, power that was useful to him in his political activities. Power over the peasants who worked Candido's land, over the shepherds, over the cowherds. From another point of view, it must be said, too, that he could never have dared even to try to rob his grandson. The brothers and sisters of Candido's father had attempted to obtain guardianship of their brother's son, who had been the cause of that brother's death. Since they had not obtained it, they lay in wait, ready to pounce upon the General if he were found in the slightest wanting. They had also tried, and were still trying, to draw Candido into the orbit of their affection for him, which, they protested, was deep and enduring, yet Candido, monster that he seemed also to them, turned a deaf ear, monster that he was. Nonetheless the General feared an alliance between Candido and his paternal relatives, and this gave Candido power over the General.

Accordingly, the threat to remove Candido from Archpriest Lepanto's afterschool tutoring could not be carried out if Candido himself decisively opposed it. As he did decisively oppose it after the 1953 elections, in which the General managed to be re-elected, but in tenth place. The reason for his slip to tenth place was, according to the General, the Archpriest's hostility toward him, which hostility had been caused by Candido's turning informer and the subsequent clash between the General and the Archpriest.

Seeing himself downgraded from first place in the 1948 elections to tenth in those of 1953, the General foamed with anger. On the day the results were made known, the sight of his grandson, smiling and tranquil as always, precipitated a genuine nervous attack. He insulted him in the name of loyalty, *omertà*, and love for the family he represented, sentiments that Candido did not know, nor, worm that he was, would ever know; he insulted the Archpriest in the name of other virtues, such as industry, chastity, fidelity, and anti-Communism, to which virtues the Archpriest was a stranger. At that point, Concetta, who was present at the scene, rose up. Although she disapproved of the insults to Candido, she could even bring herself to agree with them: Candido was incapable of observing the rules of right living. But the General should not permit himself to utter insults to the Archpriest, especially not those touching on his chastity, which was universally acknowledged.

The General planted himself in front of her, pointed an accusing index finger at her bosom, at her conscience, and shouted, "For whom did you vote? For whom did that rascal make you vote?" Concetta replied proudly, "I voted for the

Holy Cross, as always." But the General pressed her. "My number, did you vote for that? Tell me the truth, by all the dead who are dear to you, tell me the truth, did you vote for my number?" Concetta was rattled, and she mumbled, "That is between me and my conscience, and no one has the right to ask me." The General, sorely triumphant, trumpeted, "You did not vote for me, I know it, I know it for a fact!" Then, turning indulgent and even affectionate: "But I'm not put out, I was elected anyhow. . . . There's just one thing I would like to know. What did the Archpriest tell you to make you not vote for me?" Concetta replied, "That remains under the seal of the confessional," not realizing that she was, in effect, breaking that seal. The General turned sour. "The seal of the confessional!" he scoffed. "Idiot! Don't you realize you've just told me that it *was* he who told you not to vote for me? The seal . . ." and here he lapsed into the obscene, alluding to Concetta's unconsoled sex, unconsoled even by the Archpriest, for all of Concetta's great love.

Concetta clapped her hands over Candido's ears, that he might not hear his grandfather's indecent talk. Then she struck home: "Anyone who talks like that before a child cannot be his guardian." In his fury, the General let himself go even further. "I talk as I please! And you"—turning to Candido—"from this day forward you do not go to that rascal!" But after Concetta and Candido had gone away, the woman's threatening words began to revolve in the General's head and they calmed him down.

Meanwhile, on the way home, in exasperation Concetta broke the seal of the confessional totally. She told Candido what the Archpriest had said to her about voting: "If you really wish to vote for the Christian Democrats, choose people who may be a mite Christian." Concetta had then asked if the General was a mite Christian. "I wouldn't say so." These four words had made her uneasy, perplexed, and undecided. She had not voted for the General, but it was with some remorse. Now she felt liberated, she approved of herself, and she approved of the Archpriest. "He was right. Oh, he was so right!" And having vented her anger, her hatred for the General, having now become as hard and cold as a diamond, she drew up an inventory for Candido of his patrimony; she revealed to him the power he had over the General, she exhorted him to resist and to continue to go to the Archpriest.

Candido had no need of her exhortation: he was determined to continue his private lessons with the Archpriest. Now, however, he knew that he could make his decision stick on the basis of power that until that moment he had not realized he had. Never had he dreamed that one man could wield power over another which came from money, from land, from sheep, from cattle. And much less that he himself could have such power. When he was home, alone in his room, he wept, he did not know whether from joy or anguish. Then he went to the Archpriest's house to tell him everything, even about the weeping that had overcome him, he did not know why.

It was the first time that he had stayed to share a meal with the Archpriest. And just as it had been revealed to him that day that he was rich, so it was now revealed to him that the Archpriest was poor.

They stayed together talking until it was evening, until in the now dark room they were separated not only by the table but also by shadows; yet not exactly separated, for their voices had acquired a different afflatus, their talk a new brotherliness. Wealth, poverty . . . Evil, good . . . Possessing power, possessing none . . . The Fascism within us, the Fascism without . . . "Everything that we want to combat outside ourselves," the Archpriest said, "is inside us, and we must first look for it and fight it inside ourselves. . . . I desired wealth so much that even my wishing to become a priest came from that desire: the wealth of the Church, the wealth of the churches; the marbles, the fine stuccowork, the gilt, the embossed silver, the damasks, the silks, the embroideries heavy with gold and silver thread. . . . I knew only baroque churches, baroque in every respect. . . . You go in to hear Mass, to pray, to make confession; instead, you have entered the belly of wealth. . . . Wealth is dead but beautiful, beautiful but dead. Someone's said that, perhaps not in those exact words. And I believe that men who know themselves somewhat, who live and are conscious of living, are divided into two big categories: there are those who know that wealth is dead but beautiful and those who know that wealth is beautiful but dead. It is all a matter of revolving two words around a 'but.' . . . For me, wealth is still beautiful but more and more dead, more and more death. The problem is, can one ever reach the point where this death no longer tempts us, a point where we manage to separate beauty from death? Perhaps that point doesn't exist, but we must look for it." For Candido, this was mysterious discourse, but he felt the mystery had something to do with truth, with a truth so luminous and suspended that it seemed to him it would have been dispelled had he ventured, for example, to ask what a baroque church was.

The Archpriest had greatly changed in the three years that had passed since Candido began to visit him. The General lamented his having advised the faithful not to vote for him; many others lamented the fact that he had not attended to the elections as he had in 1948, that instead he had sowed doubt and uncertainty among Catholics. And furthermore, he persisted in marrying Communists in church, baptizing their children, tolerating red flags at funerals, notwithstanding the fact that Communists must be considered excommunicated. Greatly, greatly changed: so much so that he no longer thought of urging that the bishop's imprimatur be granted his essay on moral psychology. Candido was aware of the change: he saw the Archpriest become less active, wearier, more self-absorbed, more indifferent. But he did not understand that in part this change was attributable to him, because for his sake and in his own behalf the Archpriest had been slowly, inadvertently assuming a different responsibility toward life: different from what he had felt it to be earlier in his ministry. More human, more direct, more concerned and sustained.

That evening, in any event, the much labored decision to which both came was this: it was impossible to prevent the General's fearing that Candido might change sides, that he might turn to paternal relatives for a better guardianship, availing himself also of the Archpriest's protection and of Concetta's henceforth proud enmity for the General; however, Candido would neither do nor threaten anything to feed such a fear in his grandfather. "A hypocritical decision," the Archpriest commented, but one that reduced to a minimum the curse of power for someone who, like Candido, now knew that he possessed it.

About the mysterious crime, the author of which
Candido and the Archpriest happened to discover,
and about the condemnation both received from
the entire city, and the Archpriest from
the hierarchy as well

A parish priest, serving in the city's newest church in its newest neighborhood, had been murdered: in the sacristy, shortly after the bells of that church had rung for the Ave Maria; by whom was not known, nor was any motive of revenge or robbery immediately apparent. In the church there was nothing to steal, or very little, and nothing was missing. And the parish priest, apart from the usual electioneering, seemed incapable of having done anything that would cause someone to want to kill him. Police and Carabinieri were groping for clues. The bishop wrote a sorrowful letter to the Archpriest, and expressed the hope that so ferocious a crime against a *sacerdos* of the Church of Christ not go unpunished.

A police inspector arrived from the capital; before beginning his investigation, he wanted to speak with the Archpriest about the case. Candido was at the rectory when the inspector arrived. The inspector tried more than once to get the Archpriest to send Candido away, but the idea had suddenly occurred to the Archpriest to see how Candido would react to the scene, whether it would remind him of another many years before. If Candido had inside some clotted and obscure feeling, this could be the moment when he might free himself of it. He invited the inspector to speak freely, as

48

if Candido were not there, and at the same time offered the assurance that the boy would not disclose a single word of their conversation to anyone. Not convinced, and indeed feeling rather uneasy, the inspector began to speak. He related everything that there was to relate: coroner's report, depositions.

The priest had been murdered shortly after the sacristan had rung the Ave bell: an important detail, because immediately after ringing it, the sacristan tried to enter the sacristy to tell the priest that he had to run home for a moment; however, contrary to the usual practice, the door was locked from within. Inside, the priest was talking with someone. The sacristan knocked. The priest asked, "What do you want?" And the sacristan: "Nothing. I just want to tell you that I'm going home for a minute." And the priest: "All right, but make it really a minute." And he went on talking with the other person.

The sacristan confessed to having stayed for a moment to eavesdrop. He heard the other man speak. He recognized the voice of the lawyer ———. "I'm not mentioning the name," the inspector said, "because it isn't fair to mix him up in this business. In any case, it's been checked out, and he's got nothing to do with it." When the sacristan returned half an hour later, he found the door still closed. He listened a bit: silence; so the lawyer had gone away. He tried the doorknob; the door opened; inside, it was dark, so dark that he stumbled over the priest's body. Murdered: three bullets—one would have been enough, each was so well placed—from a revolver that the experts had identified as German, from the war; a model that until only a few years earlier could be found in local markets.

When the lawyer was questioned, he replied tranquilly that the sacristan could have heard his voice only in his dreams:

on the evening in question, he had not left his house, busy as he was studying a case that he had to argue in court the following day. He had gone many times to see the priest, of whom he was both friend and collaborator (he was a director on the board of the Hospital of San Giovanni di Dio, of which the priest was president), but that particular evening, no, absolutely not. Neither the Carabinieri nor the sacristan could doubt the lawyer's word. The sacristan admitted that, beyond doubt, he had made a mistake; it was easy to make a mistake, since in the sacristy—and this was borne out by a test—voices altered somewhat; they acquired a kind of resonance. "That's all we have to go on," the inspector concluded. "In a word, nothing."

At this point, Candido said, as if to himself, "The voice."

"What about the voice?" The inspector turned toward him in irritation. He had foreseen that the boy would meddle: one of those conceited, eager-beaver, cheeky boys that priests like to have hanging around.

"Voices," Candido said tranquilly, "are almost always real."

The inspector wavered between anger and dismay. He turned to stare at the priest, his face one large question mark: a question mark that flashed from the left eye, curved over the wrinkles on his forehead, descended, thinning out and clouding the right eye with doubt, ending in a mouth open in indignant stupefaction.

The Archpriest had turned pale; he looked thinner, more gaunt, and his forehead glistened with sweat. He was filled with amazement and terror because Candido had apprehended what he was thinking, what he should say but did not want to say. After a long silence, he said, "Voices are almost always real, and things are almost always simple."

The inspector still sat as if turned to stone by his mute question. Then, as if shaking himself out of a hypnotic state, the Archpriest said, "I believe I have guessed the lawyer's name from what you have told me, but I would not like there to be any equivocation. . . . Will you be good enough to tell me what it is?" The inspector automatically, as if it were now he who had gone into a hypnotic state, told him. And the Archpriest: "Thank you . . . Excuse me, I will be back in a moment." He got up and went into the other room. Candido understood intuitively that he needed to collect himself, to pray. He returned, more serene. He said simply, "I am sorry, but it is possible."

"What?" the inspector asked.

"That voices are almost always real and things almost always simple."

Not understanding and not wanting to understand, the inspector stammered. "You mean . . . you mean . . ."

"Exactly," the Archpriest said.

"But why?"

"That you will not learn from me," the Archpriest said firmly.

The inspector learned it, in fact, from others and, all things considered, without too much trouble. He learned it, in the end, from the lawyer himself. He had gone to the priest in one final attempt to prevail upon him to marry his daughter, a girl of eighteen, who had been seduced by the priest and was expecting a child. But the priest had assumed such a negative and scornful attitude as to deserve those three well-aimed bullets. After more than a week, the lawyer felt not a shadow of remorse; as a lawyer, he had only one preoccupation: to present as many witnesses as he could to testify that he always carried the revolver with him, that he had not armed himself with the premeditation of committing murder. For that matter, the entire city endorsed his act virtually to the point of acclamation for dual reasons: he had avenged his honor and he had avenged it upon a priest. A sudden eruption of anticlericalism, like a volcano so long quiet that it had seemed dead, inflamed the town. And since everybody knew how things had happened, that it had been Candido and the Archpriest who had delivered the author of that crime into the clutches of the police, the bishop was not long in knowing it, too. He assigned a learned theologian to conduct an inquiry into the case. The outcome of this inquiry was that an invitation, at first veiled, then explicit, was addressed to the Archpriest that he step down as archpriest: he could not continue to fulfill that office if all the faithful now disapproved of him, even despised him. "And further," the learned theologian said, "not that truth may not be beautiful, but at times it does so much harm that to withhold it is not a fault but a merit."

In handing the theologian his resignation, the Archpriest, now archpriest no longer, said, in a parodying, almost lilting voice, " 'I am the way, the truth, and the life,' but sometimes I am the blind alley, the lie, and death."

The theologian took this in ill part. But the ex-Archpriest's state of mind was almost jubilant.

*About the attempt the ex-Archpriest made to
dedicate himself to cultivating his own garden,
and Candido his land; and about their
disappointments therefrom*

Candido garnered a measure of respect from his schoolmates:
they looked on him as if he had been an actor in a murder
movie. The ex-Archpriest garnered respect from no one.

What with an affair that had aroused the city to indignation and provoked the bishop to the point of demoting Archpriest Lepanto, it seemed to the General that he had reached
his limit. He wrote to his daughter about the scandal, about
the scandalous behavior of Candido and Lepanto: Was it not
the occasion, now, to return to the old and right—he under-
lined *right*—idea of sending Candido to America? Maria
Grazia's reply was harsh and incisive. Whose great idea
had it been to entrust Candido to Archpriest Lepanto? Not
hers, certainly; she had always respected priests, mistrusting
them the while. So, let the General see to separating Candido
from the ex-Archpriest. As for bidding him join her in America, that was impossible: apart from Candido's reaction and
the trauma it would cause him, did her father think it possible
that a boy of thirteen, who had spent all his life in Sicily,
could arrive in the bosom of a peaceful, almost happy American family without throwing it into turmoil?

The General replied, threatening to give up his guardianship of Candido, but Maria Grazia knew he would never
give it up; she stood firm. She did promise that she would

make a quick trip to Sicily. And she did come, by surprise, many months later, at a time when Candido, in the company of the ex-Archpriest, naturally, had gone to Lourdes as a stretcher-bearer on a train of invalids, cripples, and blind who were seeking a miracle. But about this trip, which greatly edified Candido's mother when she learned of it and led her to find the General's judgment unjust and his worries exaggerated, we shall say more later.

Meanwhile, the ex-Archpriest—whom from now on we shall call Don Antonio, as Candido called him—had moved out of the rectory attached to the cathedral and into the house, unoccupied for years, that he had inherited from his father. Crucifix, inkwell, and books now lay on a wobbly little table. The house was small and damp, but it had a garden, now taken over by nettles. Don Antonio set about stubbornly to cultivate it in order to get the little he needed, as he said, to live on. He found the rusted and rickety tools that had been his father's, and he set to work, helped sometimes by Candido. In sowing and transplanting, manuring, hoeing, and pruning, he relied on the memory of what, in years long gone by, he had seen his father do; but either memory failed him or the soil, the air, the succession of rain and sun, the round of the seasons had changed, because for him everything came up sickly and stunted. He was not discouraged, however; he believed that, as with everything in life that bore fruit, it was a question of love: he had not yet arrived at loving fully that soil and that labor.

Don Antonio's garden reminded Candido that he owned land. He went to see his fields, and he took a kind of inventory: how extensive they were, how many people worked them, what crops they bore, how many cattle and sheep grazed on them. A lot of land, and very few people working it; almost everyone had gone to Belgium, France, Venezuela;

the few who remained were dispirited, not only by age but also by the flight of their children to those faraway lands. If the children had gone away, if it was unlikely that they would ever return, what sense did it make for them to go on working the land?

Candido asked the General's permission to attend to his properties. The General granted it, but on condition that Candido not ask him for money for tools, machinery, or improvements. "The way things are going," he said, "you still get something out of it. If you try to do anything new, there'll be no more profit and presently no more land." Candido said that he would not ask him for money for farm implements or improvements; he only wanted to go to work on his land himself. However, in order to go and come more quickly than on his bicycle, he needed a motorcycle. The General's consent was prompt, even generous; he advised him to get one of the most powerful models, perhaps in the hope that he would break his neck. The deduction is ours, not Candido's. Candido simply believed that such generosity on the part of his guardian was a reward for his never having asked for money beyond the small change his grandfather gave him every month. Furthermore, Candido used the motorcycle prudently, not fancying its speed or its roar. He went out into the country, did his two or three hours of hoeing, and came back: quietly, regularly. He had chosen for himself a piece of land near a spring and had prepared and manured the earth well— manured it so well that what he sowed came up burned. He worked on the basis of what he read in a farming handbook, what he saw Don Antonio doing, and what the peasants advised. They had never seen the General out in the fields; as a result, in a way they respected him and were devoted to him. The women and some of the old men even gave him their votes; the others solemnly promised to vote for him, and then swore that they had, but instead voted for the Communist Party. Candido, who went out to work on the land every day, they detested. It seemed to them that he was coming to spy on them, to harass them. And it seemed to them also that his working on the land, which they viewed as a pastime or a whim, was a parody of their work, a scoffing, a mockery. Candido believed, instead, that they were pleased to see him, to talk with him, just as he was pleased to be with them, to listen to their pithy speech, their stories, their parables. He also performed services for them, bringing things they needed from town. But nothing succeeded in making a dent in their ancient hatred of the master; a hatred that the General's absence had allowed to subside but that Candido's continued presence vigorously rekindled. What's more, Candido struck them as a kind of usurper, a thief. Not only as the master always was in relation to them and their labor but also in relation to the property of the lawyer Munafò, God rest him (an insupportable master when alive, a good soul, God rest him, when dead and for dying in that fashion): property that could not be, and was not, Candido's by right since it was to him, precisely, that the poor lawyer owed his passage to the state of being a good soul.

Candido, as we have said, was unaware of the peasants' hatred, but discomfort at being the master of that land he did feel. Why should all those fields be his? How was it that a man—his grandfather or his great-grandfather—who had never worked them, or had worked only a tiny part of them, had made them all his own? And was it right for him to receive them as he had received them, and to keep them for himself? These were questions that he put to himself and put also to the peasants; and when they heard these questions put to them, the peasants hated him all the more. Yet the answers they gave him were of this kind: you work, and what you make you make for your sons, and it is right that your sons and the sons of your sons keep it, enjoy it, and hand it down intact along the line of your descendants. And they really did think this, but did not do so in relation to Candido, who had fallen heir to all those things and all that land by virtue of a legitimacy that had nothing to do with the true kind. For them, true legitimacy was the resemblance, almost the identical likeness, of son to father, the son's living by the father's rules, the son's not betraying the father whether he was right or wrong (especially not, in fact, when he was wrong). And then, that talk about the land belonging to the peasants, the land belonging to the people who work it, they were good and tired of that talk; for the sake of that mirage, they had backed the Communist Party, and they still backed it, but wearily, without believing in it, without wanting it. "The land is tired," they would say, "and we are more tired than it is." Candido used to imagine that if he ceded his lands to the peasants, and he proposed to do so as soon as the law allowed it, their emigrant sons would return, and all the fields that lay uncultivated, abandoned to grass and brush, would become neat, tidy, productive once more. But one day when he was making this speech to the peasants, he was told that their sons would return, yes, but to sell the land and go back to where they now lived. They said this to him with scorn for him and for the land.

Candido was disappointed; he lost his enthusiasm, he realized that there was something ridiculous in his wish to play peasant. He enjoyed the work; it gave him a healthy fatigue, a healthy appetite, healthy sleep; but, in addition to his sense of its being ridiculous, he began to be worried by the fact that he enjoyed it as a privilege: the ancient privilege of the master, which once took the form of income and now the almost sportive pleasure of clumsily cultivating a patch of garden.

He and Don Antonio talked about this at length. They did not want to resign themselves to defeat. And before defeat definitely arrived, Don Antonio had the idea of the pilgrimage to Lourdes. "You will see how much good it does us," he said mysteriously to Candido, as if he were talking about a tonic or detoxifying cure.

About the journey that Candido and Don Antonio
made to Lourdes, and about the good that
it did them both

Don Antonio had already been to Lourdes, in the summer of 1939, shortly before war broke out. He had been as old then as Candido was now. To go back there after almost twenty years would be a sort of split experience for him; his impressions would be divided between those he had had of Lourdes at fifteen, which would be verified and in a sense relived through Candido, and those he would now experience. But there was this difference: before, he had been a seminarian full of fears and shame about sin; full of pimples that made him believe they were and that he really did believe were a sign of sin; full of devotion for the Madonna in which he submerged himself so as to be cleansed of sin; whereas Candido was utterly averse to believing that there were any sins other than lying and seeking the pain and humiliation of others, and he felt no devotion for images of the Madonna and of the Saints unless they were well painted or sculpted—and even then it was not a matter of devotion but of admiration and pleasure.

Although urged more than once by Candido, Don Antonio never was willing to say a word about his earlier impressions. We can say, however, that they had been fairly liberating with regard to an obsessive preoccupation with sinning and a no less obsessive devotion to the Madonna;

furthermore, from those impressions he had derived a measure of practicality and skill that in a short time had advanced him from chaplain to parish priest, and from parish priest to archpriest in a career that was now abruptly closed to him. And we can say this also: Don Antonio was making his new trip to Lourdes with the intention of obtaining from it a definitive liberation.

They left Palermo in the afternoon during a tremendous sirocco. Because the train that brought them to Palermo had been late, Don Antonio and Candido arrived when the special train for Lourdes was ready to depart. They were scolded by the lady who appeared to be in charge of the large company and by the priest who was assisting her, especially Candido, who, as a stretcher-bearer, should have been there at least two hours early. But the reproof, severe in substance, in tone and choice of words was charitable, almost imploring. Candido was upset by it. Had it not been for Don Antonio, he would perhaps have gone back home. Perhaps: for the desire to make that journey—his first—was like a fever in him, anxious, visionary, slightly delirious.

Further distress awaited him when he walked through the first coach: those crutches propped against the seats, those suffering faces turned toward him, those sightless eyes. A distress, however, that did not make him regret in the slightest having undertaken the journey but, rather, quickened his amazement and admiration that it was possible to bring together and organize so much human suffering in a convoy of hope. In that sum of suffering, in that organization and exhibition of bodily misfortunes, there was something both repugnant and grandiose. At first it was the grandiosity that Candido sensed, while Don Antonio was visibly assailed by repugnance: what had been scarcely more than a flash of repugnance on his first trip had since been deepened through recollection and reflection, and was now fully confirmed. Not because of those bodies, those sores, those watery or white eyes, those slaverings, but because of that organized, convoyed hope.

In the two days that it took to reach Lourdes, Candido's amazement and admiration gave way to repugnance. He talked about other things with Don Antonio, and Don Antonio with him. Only, at one point Candido did not restrain himself from saying, "If I were God, I would be offended by all this," and Don Antonio assented, nodding his head and smiling wearily. Yet as a counterpoint to his repugnance—and this could be observed in the other stretcher-bearers, the nurses, the sisters, the priests—there was in him a kind of physical exaltation, a euphoria, almost a celebration of good health, of appetites, of desires. During the first hours of the trip, the daughters and the married women of good families who were acting as nurses had seemed stiffened and transfixed in a voluntary mortification of themselves and of their bodies, as they habitually were in their daily lives; but as night fell, they acquired a freedom, a bursting vitality, a nascent, blossoming carnality until even the ugly ones looked beautiful. The stretcher-bearers and priests must have made the same, or a similar, impression on the nurses and sisters, to judge from the tremulous, joyous eagerness in their voices, the warbling words they exchanged, and their luminous, vaguely ecstatic glances. And there had to happen, there could not but happen in the Manichean world—illness/health—which the train had become, what did happen to Candido the second night. At dawn of the second day, he had awakened and, as he had on the first day, had stepped out into the corridor. There, walking ahead of him, was a nurse; when the train suddenly lurched, Candido felt her press and then weigh upon him as if the wall against which he was leaning had become the floor. Instinctively, he reached out to prevent her falling, to support her above him; and it was as if the train had remained coupled to that brusque motion, that suspension. Through his clothing he felt himself groped after, then avidly sought out beneath his clothing, and he never did know if it was one moment before or one moment after or at the same moment that he began to trace her body outside her clothing, to grope after her, to seek her. The intensity with which his hands were sensing gave him, in a flash, an image of himself as blind: that body was limpidly designed in his mind only through the signs that touch transmitted. They kissed long, long. Then Candido felt and, in his profound and most sweet blindness, saw himself and the world become a sphere of liquid iridescence, of music.

The girl drew away from him, and walked silently down the half-dark corridor. She turned before disappearing, and so Candido was able to recognize her later. She was not beautiful, although she could not be called ugly. Had the journey lasted, to Candido she would have been most beautiful. But in the hours that remained and during the return trip, her glance swept over him so indifferently that it made him wonder whether he had been mistaken, whether he had lived that moment of love with another person. Don Antonio reassured him, not because he knew the girl but because he knew the world of Catholic charity, and also those acts of fugitive love, of sin, like the opening and closing of the blooms called moonflowers, which were part of it. From that trip to Lourdes, which was otherwise distressing and depressing, Candido retained this joy, this revelation, this miracle. Of the whole trainload, he was the one miraculously healed person. Don Antonio had programed the trip for Candido as a vaccination against Catholicism, and for himself as a salute, a farewell, a good-bye. But, notwithstanding the variation that befell Candido, the balance was still on the credit side. Candido could consider himself not only vaccinated but immune. And he himself was entirely cured, released, free.

About the love for women, and for one woman,
by which Candido was seized, and about what
Don Antonio had to say to him in this regard

On their return from Lourdes, Don Antonio was no longer a priest. He wanted Candido to call him simply Antonio, but now and then the "Don" slipped out (as it does also with us). Antonio had grown so lighthearted, gay, and witty as to seem cynical and blasphemous to anyone who was not witty. "I have been cynical, I have been blasphemous, and now that I am so no longer, these are the vices they accuse me of," he said. Often he declared that he had become very religious. As proof of the religiosity he had finally achieved, he pointed to the blooming of his garden: now that the earth felt him to be a living man, it responded to his passion. Candido was not totally convinced of this: the poor earth was finally responding to more experienced and knowledgeable labor. He could not help thinking, however, that what Don Antonio said about the earth might do well for woman, for women; on the train to Lourdes, he had learned that love responds to love. And because he felt that experience was slipping away like a dream, becoming every day more form-less, vaguer, he wished to repeat it, he had but one idea, which was to repeat it, to confirm it, to complete it. He used to speak about this to Don Antonio, since he was accustomed to speak to him about everything freely, without impediment or shame.

"You see," Don Antonio would say, "women belong to

my past as a priest. To really love them, or to love one of them, I would have to free myself of that past. It was a long illness, and now I am convalescing. It's easy to knock down all the dogmas, simulacra, and symbols that have been part of your life, one after another, as if you were in a shooting gallery. I'd say that if your eye is not too dim, the little carbine that is Voltaire's *Dictionary* would be enough. But all those dogmas and simulacra and symbols you believe you have knocked down are going to gather themselves together and hide in the body of woman, in the idea of love, or simply in the act of making love. I feel myself so deeply in the truth—in every thing, every thought—that at moments it seems to me I have crossed the threshold of the secret, of the mystery; and that is, there is no secret, there is no mystery; everything is simple, inside us and outside. But to love or to make love in this simplicity, or on the borders of it, would not be possible for me, I believe, nor would it please me. And however free one may run, I believe that the Church, the Churches—those that exist now, those that will come later—will have the better of it. Between the epistles of Saint Paul and Stendhal's *De l'amour* the discourse runs along the same thread of fire: the hell of the other world, the hell of this one. And it is a splendid discourse."

"But love is simple," Candido said.

"Not for me," Don Antonio said. "The hell of love continues to be my paradise."

Of the simplicity of love, the earthly paradise with no divine prohibitions or diabolic temptations, Candido was to make further proof, but this time he would skirt another's hell.

We have neglected until now to say that the General, a widower from before the war in Spain, had a woman who kept house for him and was therefore known as his house-keeper. Not always the same woman: from '38 on, he had changed his housekeeper four or five times, each one being younger than the last, in step with his advancing age, so that the last in charge could be said to be very young indeed. She had been with him for several years. Exemplary in her management of the house, absolutely the best the General had had: this by the General's own statement and judging by the hatred for her that Concetta did not conceal. To have to admit that "that woman" (so Concetta called her) knew how to keep the house spotless and tidy to a degree un-known to Concetta, that she knew how to cook (this one gathered from the odors that arose from the kitchen), that the General's shirts were well ironed was for Concetta an anguish that found solace in the fact, for her absolutely certain, that "that one" came from one of the unmentionable houses now abolished by law. For her, there was no doubt that "that one" went to bed with the General. In all truth, no such doubt was nourished by anyone who knew the General and had seen the housekeeper. Except for Candido, who had never paid any attention to Concetta's hints. For almost two years, the housekeeper had been invisible for him: she was one of those people who are relegated to the status of objects that are there, that cannot *not* be there, but the habit of seeing them there is such that one no longer sees them, and they begin to exist only when they truly are there no longer. Furthermore, this person seemed to wish to make herself in-visible: she dressed anonymously, she spoke little, she dis-appeared when anyone called on the General. Whether she was young or middle-aged, blond or dark, shapely or thin, Candido, if asked all of a sudden, would have been unable to say. This until the summer afternoon when, as he was

66

reading Marx, he saw on the page two gray-blue eyes, a lock of blond hair, the curve of a mouth, a fluid line descending from bosom to thigh: a painting barely sketched, one to be completed.

He closed the book, got up, left the house, and went—he who for months had not set foot in his grandfather's house—to complete the image that had appeared to him. He was so taken by that image that not for a moment did he think of the General or calculate the chances of his being away (probability fifty percent, usually, but in the summer, when Parliament was in recess, twenty-five).

The General was in Rome, she told Candido when he came to the house. She was a little sleepy; tying the belt of her dressing gown, her hands were slow and uncertain. She did not ask him what he wanted; she moved toward the sitting room, and Candido followed, his glance gently brushing over her body, which was outlined and visible under the light material of her robe, and her movements, which, from her step to the raising of her hands to adjust her hair, were like the slow commencement of a dance.

In the almost dark sitting room, she turned to look at him; her eyes were laughing, even if her mouth pouted. She drew a handkerchief from the pocket of her dressing gown and passed it lightly over her lips and eyelids. It slipped, or she allowed it to slip, from her hand. It glided down onto the rug. "Candide picked it up; she innocently held his hand; the young man innocently kissed the young lady's hand with remarkable vivacity, tenderness, and grace; their lips met, their eyes sparkled, their knees trembled, their hands wandered."

Unlike his namesake, whose adventures and misadventures had come off the presses of Lambert two hundred years earlier, Candido's pleasure that day was long, full, and peaceful. A pleasure long, fully, and peacefully shared by Paola. And likewise in the days and months that followed, for almost a year passed before the General, alerted by an anonymous letter, caught them.

About the Communism of Candido and of Don
Antonio, and about the discussions that they
had with each other and with comrades

Candido, then, was reading Marx. First he had read Gramsci, then Lenin; now he was reading Marx. He was bored with Marx, but he persevered. Gramsci's books, on the other hand, he had read with great interest, and also with emotion, as he imagined that small, frail, ailing man devouring books and annotating them with his own reflections: in this way, Gramsci had conquered both Fascism and the prison in which Fascism had kept him. It seemed to Candido that he could see him, see the cell, the table, the notebook, the hand writing; that he could hear the light scratching of the nib against the paper. He talked often with Don Antonio about Gramsci and whatever work of Gramsci's he had just been reading. But Don Antonio did not care much for Gramsci; he saw an error, a fissure creeping through the pages of the *Notebooks*. Italian Catholics: Where had Gramsci seen them? On Sundays, at midday Mass—since they did not otherwise exist. They were a weakness, and Gramsci had begun to make them into a force in the history of Italy, in the country's future. "Let's hope the error doesn't grow, the fissure does not lengthen," he used to say. But it seemed to Candido that on this subject Don Antonio was not sufficiently well balanced. From his having been a priest he retained too much disappointment, too much resentment, and therefore what he had been might be unduly influencing what he now wished to be.

Candido had been bored with Lenin, too, but differently than with Marx and to a lesser degree. He had come to picture Lenin as a carpenter atop a scaffolding who had worn himself out hitting the same nails on the head, but all of his efforts had not prevented some nails from being poorly set or going in crooked.

He had emerged from the pages of Lenin as if from the din of a shipyard, and he had moved on into the pages of Marx exactly as when, after visiting a shipyard, one goes into the office of the man who directs it. And just as it is not easy for everyone, and is hard for most, to read the graphs, the plans, the elevations affixed all over the walls, so Candido felt that he was wandering about in the pages of Marx without knowing how to read them. This impression, this unease stayed with him until, after reading everything by Marx that he could find, he went back and reread *The Communist Manifesto*. Then it was clear to him that perhaps he had indeed not known how to read many things, but others he had not understood precisely because he had understood them; that is, he had denied that Marx had meant to say and had said precisely what he had said. When Candido had studied Machiavelli in school, he had been much impressed; that is to say, he had come to wonder whether Machiavelli was intelligent, and how he could have believed in a future in which firearms would be set aside in favor of a return to cold steel. What Marx was proposing in relation to that great and simple truth about capital, about capitalism, might, Candido thought, be of the same order as Machiavelli's forecast of a return to steel weapons. Was it not possible even then, Candido asked himself, to see that capitalism would have the choice between swords and guns? And how was it possible not to understand that capitalism would opt for firearms and would make them ever more murderously efficient?

It was a thought—both a conjecture and a question—that he was reluctant and afraid to express even in front of Don Antonio during the discussions they were always having about their being Communists and about the basic texts of Communism. For Candido, being a Communist was a simple fact, like being thirsty and wanting to drink; to him the texts did not matter much. For Don Antonio, it was a very complicated, very subtle matter, all pinpointed on an apparatus of referrals to the texts, of glosses. Certain statements that eluded him Candido was unable to explain well to himself, much less was he capable of demonstrating them as theorems to Don Antonio. So it happened that whenever he felt Don Antonio was not in agreement and might ask him to make a demonstration, he would clam up as if he were already worsted, even if he did not feel worsted. Once when he happened to remark that, compared to Lenin and Marx, Victor Hugo and Zola and even Gorki "were better," Don Antonio said, in almost angry astonishment, "What does that mean, they're 'better'? In what sense are they 'better'?" Although what he felt was to him quite clear, Candido expressed it with difficulty and effort: they "were better" because they talked about things that still *are*, while Marx and Lenin, well, it was as if they talked about things that *are* no longer. "Zola and Gorki, they talk about things that used to be, and it's as if they were talking about things that came later. Marx and Lenin talk about things that would happen, and it's as if they were talking about things that are no longer." This was not enough for Don Antonio; he pursued his questioning, and Candido did not know what to answer except to say that if he had read only Marx and Lenin he would not be a Communist, or he would be only if it meant something like going to a masquerade as a Communist—dressed up as in the days of Marx, as in the days of Lenin. To Don Antonio the reply seemed born of some confusion Candido must have built up in himself, and Candido was unable to say more to clarify for Don Antonio what he himself saw most clearly.

To be a Communist was, in a word, almost a fact of nature for Candido: capitalism was bearing man toward dissolution, toward the end; the instinct to conserve, the will to survive found expression in Communism. Communism, in a word, was something that had to do with love, also with making love: in Paola's bed, in the General's house. This Don Antonio understood and, generally and generically, he approved; but with regard to himself, to his being a Communist, he had a different idea. "A priest who is no longer a priest," he used to say, "either marries or he becomes a Communist. One way or the other, he must continue to stand on the side of hope, but in one way or the other, not in both ways." Candido did not understand. Don Antonio explained. "Someone who has not been a priest can have a family and he can be a Communist. Indeed, one might think having a family would be one more reason for his being a Communist. I say one *might* think so because, in fact, at a certain point the family will inevitably end up weighing more on the side of conservation than on that of revolution. But if someone has been a priest and no longer is because he came to feel that his ministry had been reduced to the role of a dead man burying other dead and if this man then becomes a Communist, he cannot run the risk twice of no longer wanting to conserve. Otherwise, he might as well have gone on being a priest. The celibacy that the Church still imposes on priests is the single revolutionary thing remaining in the Church, but by now it's a mere formality." Candido still did not understand. Or, rather, he did not wish to understand, for at times he was assailed by the apprehension that Don Antonio was passing from one church to another. He once went so far as to tell Don Antonio this, causing him great worry and fret.

They wanted to join the Party, but the Party, particularly in the person of the Honorable di Sales, did not appear inclined to welcome them. If Don Antonio had been one of those priests who leave the Church after a long or noisy quarrel with the hierarchy, his joining the Party would have been hailed as a significant event. But he had left after being demoted, after accepting his demotion, and in silence. Also, popular he was not, because of his having sent to jail that poor lawyer who had redeemed the honor of his own daughter and of his family by killing a very bad priest (which, to most people's way of thinking, was tantamount to saying "a priest like all other priests" and like Don Antonio himself). As for Candido, a host of reasons argued against admitting him to the Party: among them, his having a mother who had gone off with an American officer who had had the whole city under his thumb and had favored Fascists and mafiosi; his being the grandson of a Fascist general who had become a Demo-Christian deputy; and his being rich. Less rich than the Honorable di Sales, but rich. Ergo, there was much beating about the bush when they asked to be admitted into the Party. They were accepted only when the Party (which is to say, the Honorable di Sales) presently realized how many young Communists, both students and workers, were beginning to form a circle around Don Antonio and Candido.

Almost every evening, these young people were to be found at Don Antonio's house. It had all begun one evening when Candido brought with him to Don Antonio's his only school companion who was also a friend: poor, intelligent, and Communist. He became the first link in a chain of friendship, of solidarity, which Don Antonio was able to forge and extend thanks to a spontaneous heart and the skills of an ex-priest. To make a living, Don Antonio was giving private lessons and helping young men who had no idea of even where to start writing a paper prepare theses for their degrees (in Italian literature, Latin literature, philosophy). In the evening, he would lead discussion groups with young Communists, which were like a kind of school. This worried the Honorable di Sales; at the same time, these same young people were putting pressure on him for Don Antonio and Candido to be admitted into the Party. So he came to a decision: he would allow them to join, but he bade his most trusted fellow-members keep an eye on the pair and bring them up on charges at the first sign of heterodoxy. He requested Don Antonio to move the evening meetings from his house to Party headquarters; and thus Party headquarters became a kind of night school, but free and freely improvised, where the talk was about Marxism and psychoanalysis, about world affairs and domestic affairs.

But it could not last. And, in fact, it did not last.

About how the General became enraged with Candido
and Paola, and about Paola's going to live in
Candido's house, and the consequent
flight of Concetta

As we have said, an anonymous letter warned the General that his housekeeper and his grandson "lay with each other in his absence." This was the exact phrase, and if only the General had thought about it for a moment, he would have been in a position to recognize the author of the letter, as would almost all the town's inhabitants had they seen it. The writer was a municipal employee, one Scalabrino, who was an assiduous reader of Boccaccio and a no less assiduous, always anonymous, certifier to sexual and administrative misdemeanors. But the moment the General read the letter, he was in no condition to reflect, being torn in his pride between the wish to be unaware or not to believe, and the wish to know. The latter prevailed, to his loss: he surprised them, Candido and Paola, as they "lay together." He called Candido a cad and Paola a tart, he shouted that he would kill them, and rushed from the room, still shouting that they deserved to die and that die they would. Paola and Candido thought that he might have run to snatch a rifle or a revolver from his panoply and that he might reappear to shoot them down. But they had time to dress and still the General did not appear. Nor could they hear him. They were seized by a fear greater than that of seeing him reappear armed. Silently, cautiously, they went to look for him.

75

The General was in the sitting room, motionless in an armchair, as if he had fallen into it; his eyes were clouded. Without stirring, he said, "Out! Both of you, get out of here at once, and never let me see your faces again!" Candido felt sorry, Paola a little less so. They went out, Paola just as she was, in a dressing gown. Had Scalabrino been lying in ambush in the vicinity of the General's house, he would have had the satisfaction of recording the effect of his letter. But although Scalabrino was not there, although the street seemed deserted at that hour, many invisible spectators witnessed that departure. As well as Concetta's departure from Candido's house, one hour later. The moment Concetta saw "that woman" appear before her, together with Candido, both of them white-faced, "that woman" wearing only a dressing gown and already turning into "this woman," she sensed confusedly and then knew for certain what had happened. When Candido said firmly that Paola had come to stay with them, Concetta uttered a piercing shriek, crossed herself, and, still shrieking, said that where "this woman" stayed, she could not remain. She snatched her belongings from the closets, furiously bundled them up, lifted them to her shoulder, and left, cursing as she went down the stairs and as far as the great door against "this woman," Candido, the ex-Archpriest—lost souls, all three of them. She went to the house of the General, as if the most just and obvious thing was for her to go there and for the General to welcome her. For hours, they did not speak; then, upon the General's invitation that she go to sleep in the room that had been "that woman's," Concetta disdainfully refused, saying she preferred the tiniest cubbyhole to that large, comfortable room irremediably and for all time contaminated by the sins of "that woman." She then uncorked everything that was fermenting within her. Hatred for "that woman" and for the ex-Arch-

76

priest, both of them damned, equally damned: he for having tempted and corrupted Candido in the mind, she in the body; remorse in regard to the General, for not having given him her vote and for not having trusted him when he had said that the then Archpriest was a rascal even before, *even before* he had been demoted and had given up his priesthood; pity for Candido, now ruined, now lost; commiseration for herself and for the General, both unworthily betrayed by two beings who had fallen into the abyss of bestiality (but Candido through the fault of "that woman"). Both betrayed, yet if one wished to be fair, the General deservedly, she undeservedly. "How is it that a man like you goes and brings a woman like that into his own house?" The General made a weary gesture of protest. "Let's not begin that. If there are any reproaches to be made, I make them myself. That's enough. . . . Now, go to sleep."

"To sleep?" Concetta was dumbfounded. "How can a person sleep when such things happen? . . . We should be talking; we should be talking until tomorrow." And indeed they did talk until dawn. So began the General's new life.

As for Candido, the regret he felt for the General's sake and the sharper regret he felt for Concetta did not prevent his making love with Paola, who was dazed by freedom, by happiness. Until dawn.

About the warnings Candido received from the
Party, and about how the first steps were taken
to build a case against him

The city was long abuzz over all that had happened that day
between the house of the General and that of Candido. The
facts were properly integrated, then elaborated and spiced
with a measure of spite. The General had had a heart attack,
according to some people; a stroke, according to others; Paola
was expecting a baby, whether the child of the General or of
Candido no one knew; the Christian Democrats had requested
the General to resign from Parliament, and the Communist
Party had asked Candido to resign from the Young Communist League. It was said, too, that Paola had been the
mistress not only of the General and of Candido but also
of Don Antonio, which brought the putative fathers of the
child she was expecting to three; it would be a delicious game
presently to determine by a citywide plebiscite to whom to
attribute paternity on the basis of resemblance.

Except for the fact that Paola had left the house of the
General and gone to Candido's, all this was pure fantasy.
There was a bit of truth in what was said about the Communist Party, which was worried about the scandal that
Candido had visited upon the entire town. The scandal was
useful, on the other hand, to the Christian Democrats, en-
abling them, in the most painless and aseptic fashion, to get
rid of the General. At the time of the last elections, they
had already tried to get rid of him by neglecting to make

78

sure that he would be re-elected; an unforeseen bloc of votes had materialized in the General's favor, which were owed, perhaps, to the unforeseeable fact that the electorate continued to appreciate honesty. The General was a stupid man, but honest; for some people, stupid insofar as he was honest, and these were precisely the people in the Christian Democrat Party who wanted to get him out from under their feet.

The Communist Party was truly worried. The young men who had supported Candido's and Don Antonio's request to be admitted to Party membership were called in one by one and severely reprimanded. Then Don Antonio was called. Then Candido was called. As if they were defendants, and must clear themselves, for what the Party had set up was a kind of pretrial hearing.

Don Antonio listened as two charges were brought against him: of not having dissuaded Candido from that love affair, that intrigue, a relationship so indecent as to verge on incest (and he could have done so, given the ascendancy he was known to have over Candido); and of having been the lover of that woman himself, according to rumors that were circulating around town. The second charge threw him into a turmoil: he was suffocated by an indignation near to nausea, and also by a grieving pity for the people who had set such rumors in motion and for those who now asked him for an accounting. Had he been able to withdraw, he would have prayed, for he still believed in God and he still prayed. Before those judges, he blushed, his eyes filled with tears, he stammered; in a word, in their eyes he behaved like a guilty man. As for the first charge, he said that he could not distinguish between love and a love affair, unless one wished to call a love affair what people had first viewed without being scandalized and had commented on with no more than amused malice: an old man's keeping a young woman for his pleasure by paying her wages. That, later, a young woman and a young man should feel attracted to each other, that they should love each other and make love, was in the order and harmony of life; it was also their business, and no one else had the right to meddle in it or to censure them. On this point a discussion broke out, which the judges abruptly cut short, affirming in the clearest and most emphatic way that the Party had every right to intervene when the private conduct of a member gave rise to gossip, even if unfounded; not to speak of scandals only too well founded, like that of Candido.

For his part, when his turn came to submit to interrogation and to clear himself, Candido said that he had never thought Paola was anything other than his grandfather's housekeeper; nor, now that they were trying to insinuate the suspicion that she might have been his grandfather's mistress, would it even enter his head to ask her about it. It was a fact that belonged to her, to her past: love if it had been love, shame if it had been shame; and if it had been shame, all the more reason for its being his duty to help her forget it and never his right to cross-examine her.

They asked him if he was willing to separate from "that woman" (for them, as for Concetta, she was "that woman"). He replied, decisively, no. They invited him to think it over, they admonished him to behave himself like someone who is waiting to be sentenced: depending upon his conduct from that moment forward, the sentence would be absolution or condemnation. Candido's impulse was to reply that he could not care less, but he kept silent, hoping that it would be they, the judges, who would think it over. Furthermore, just recently he had come of age; in terms of the law, he was a man: therefore, from now on he need answer to no one about his own life.

*About the life that Candido led between home,
the country, and the Party; and about the
proposal that was made to him and that
he did not accept*

Candido had decided to give up studying regularly, if indeed
he had ever done so. School, where he had done very well as
far as promotions and grades were concerned, had in fact
been useful to him because he read all those books that had
nothing to do with school and much to do with life. Now he
wanted to give himself completely to his land. Thanks to the
General's scrupulous management, he found that he had
money in the bank. He bought tractors, which he learned to
drive; he had ditches and trenches dug in order to make use
of the water that once went to waste; he planted vineyards
and built greenhouses for vegetables. He led the life of a
farmer and mechanic at the same time: he plowed, planted,
and grafted; he cared for the machinery, and he repaired it
when it broke down. Every evening, as dusk fell, he went home
content. And he found Paola content. Saturday evenings, or
when there was a general meeting of the membership, he
went to Party headquarters, but not every day, as when he
was going to school. He took part in the discussions, either
to bring them back to the point when they had wandered
so far afield that the point was lost to sight, or to express his
opinion in the clearest, briefest way. Especially when agri-
culture was being discussed, the few peasants who were pres-

ent always approved of his contributions, but they were almost never approved by those who sat behind the table, beneath the portraits of Marx, Lenin, and Togliatti. Every time it happened that they disapproved, Candido would return home doubting himself, his ability to see things in the right light, and sorry that he had spoken up. He found a little comfort in the fact that the peasants had approved of what he said. This was what Candido loved about the Party: being together with peasants, workers, miners: real, solid people who talked about their own needs and the city's needs in a few precise words, sometimes summarizing an entire discussion in one proverb. There was a quite sharp, even if largely unnoticed, contrast between the people who made up the Party —who in numbers, needs, and hopes *were* the Party—and those who represented and directed the Party. The speeches of the latter followed an elusive, endless trajectory; the remarks of the former were quick and dry, like shots fired at a target, and at times not without a crude irony. Don Antonio saw in this contrast, which never emerged as a contrast, however, a repetition of what had always happened and was still happening in the Church: the very people who preferred to talk little, whose family and social life was made up of silences more than of words, loved long preachments and the speakers who made themselves least understood. "My soul understands him," a little old woman had said once of a verbose and incomprehensible preacher. In their turn, then, the leaders of the Party were speaking to the souls of people who could speak and knew how to speak only of bodies.

In this mode of life, which could be called serene except for the black cloud of the judgment the Party had still to pronounce upon his conduct, Candido at a certain point found himself the leading actor in an event that was to heighten the contempt most people felt for him, and that tipped the Party's judgment away from absolution or indulgence toward condemnation.

One evening, rather late, he had a visit at home from a certain Zucco. A man of indefinable pursuits—variously a real-estate agent and a vote hustler. Candido knew him vaguely from having met him several times as his grandfather's attentive escort. In fact, he thought the man might be coming on behalf of his grandfather, not knowing that for some while Zucco, having sniffed the political odor that now emanated from the General, no longer accompanied him and, on the contrary, took pains to avoid him. Indeed, he had something quite else to speak with Candido about. He moved toward his real purpose in a roundabout way, almost as if he had come to compliment Candido on having fixed himself up with Paola and on having fixed up his properties, and then he inquired what plans Candido might have for that piece of land near the town gates which Candido perhaps did not remember he owned, since he still had not got around to fixing it up. (The expression "to fix up" was a favorite with Zucco.) Candido replied that he did remember owning it, and that perhaps he would fix it up as a vineyard. Zucco was scandalized. "Use that land for a vineyard? A vineyard on land located right by the town gates? But that land's worth gold, that land *is* gold!" And he explained how it was gold; which is to say, how it might become gold.

A plan was under consideration to build a large hospital for the city. That land was the ideal site on which to build it. Only if Candido was willing, of course. Candido replied that since it was a question of a hospital, of course he was willing; and furthermore, whether he was willing or not, the municipality or the province or the national government could always, for purposes of a public-service utility, expropriate it. "Yes, of course," Zucco said, "but the problem is money."

"I understand," Candido said, who had not understood. "Well, I can offer the land as a gift. What do you think, that I would not make a gift of the land? A hospital is so badly needed."

"Give it?" Zucco gulped.

"Yes," Candido said. "I think it can be done. A deed of gift. I'm not just sure. . . ."

"We have not understood each other," Zucco said.

"Let us try to understand each other," Candido said.

"Well . . . I . . . Let's put it this . . . Well . . ." Zucco was at a loss: he could not find the right tack to follow, the right way to talk to such an innocent babe, such a cretin as this young Munafò. His father, God rest him, would have understood like a shot. His grandfather likewise, even if he wasn't intelligent and even if he was honest (a sneer flitted across Zucco's face at the thought of the General's honesty). Who did this fellow take after, whose son was he?

Dramatic silence on the part of Zucco; an expectant pause with a touch of curiosity and some little suspicion on the part of Candido.

"The hospital," Zucco said finally, "can be built on your land or on someone else's land which is near town. Since expropriated land will bring a sky-high price, it is clear that whoever decides which site will be bought for the hospital will be doing a big favor—offering a big gift, as it were— to the owner of that land. And the owner, what does he do? Doesn't he thank whomever for that gift? He reciprocates, doesn't he?"

"He thanks how? Reciprocates how?" Candido asked. He was beginning to understand; he had assumed that drowsy-cat attitude behind which he always concealed attentiveness.

"He thanks . . . well, he reciprocates by offering a percentage of the price he'll be paid for the land. . . . Thirty percent, say, would be no more than reasonable, when you think that whoever will receive that thirty percent will see to it that the land is bought at the highest price possible."

"And who will receive this thirty percent?"

"You'll not meet anybody but me. . . . It doesn't, after all, involve just one person. There are so many, you see. . . ."

"No, I don't see," Candido said, standing up. Zucco also stood up. They looked each other in the eye.

"Signor Zucco, I will give the land," Candido said. "And now that I've thought it over, since that is the best land on which a hospital can be built, if another site is chosen I will know why, and I will press charges."

"What do you mean? You spit on a fortune like that, and you want to squeal on me, into the bargain, for bringing it to you?" And he added dismally, "Right, I should have expected as much."

"Yes, you should have expected as much," Candido said.

The next day, he went to the town hall, bringing the mayor an offer in writing to cede the land gratis. The mayor thanked him; he said that his generous offer would be carefully weighed; accepted—that he could not guarantee, of course: a technical commission would decide after due deliberation and with all due circumspection.

Candido related the whole story at the Party's next general meeting. From those who sat behind the table he received measured expressions of approval and assurances that the Party would keep an eye on how the affair progressed. A peasant got up to ask how it was that somebody, knowing Candido was a Communist, had dared make him such a proposal. "Ten years ago," he concluded, "no one would have been rash enough to go talk like that to a Communist." Ten years before, Stalin was alive: that's what the peasant was thinking, and everybody, knowing him, knew that that was what he was thinking. Some people laughed, others chided him. His question made a deep impression on Candido.

A month later, Candido learned that other land had been chosen for the hospital. He raised the question again at the next Party meeting, but in a tone that did not please those sitting behind the table. It was an accusing tone, they said, which they did not deserve and would not tolerate. They had done everything possible to have Candido's offer accepted, but technical reasons which seemed incontrovertible were against it. It would be possible, yes, to appeal to other technical experts, more expert or less interested, but that would mean everything would grind to a halt, and who knew when the city would have its hospital? "Do we want a scandal or do we want a hospital?" the members of the meeting were asked. Almost everyone wanted the hospital; Candido and a few others wanted both the hospital and the scandal. The secretary rose to speak. A long discourse about city affairs, about the Party's vision thereof, about the way in which the Party dealt with opposition, with criticism. Now and again, he struck out ironically at Candido: for his exhibitionism, his conceit, his conduct, his paying no heed to the Party's warnings.

Everyone looked at Candido each time the secretary more or less directly attacked him. Candido was altogether composed. When the secretary finished speaking, it seemed that everyone expected him to say something, so Candido said simply, "Comrade, you have been talking like Foma Fomitch." And truly this was all he had been thinking as he listened to the secretary.

86

"Like whom?" the secretary asked.

"Like Foma Fomitch."

"Ah," the secretary said. He seemed to know who Foma Fomitch was. Instead, for two days he was to rack his brains over that name.

*About the arduous inquiry that the Party
conducted to identify Foma Fomitch, and about
the conversations Candido and Don Antonio
had about this personage*

Foma Fomitch. "Carneades! Now who was he? . . . Carneades, I seem to've read or heard that name somewhere; he must be . . ." (*I promessi sposi*, Chapter 8). According to the secretary of the local Party cell, he must be someone who had something to do with the history of the Party in the Soviet Union, since surely he was Russian. Foma Fomitch. A theoretician or a security agent? "You have been talking like Foma Fomitch." Candido Munafò had certainly intended that remark, that name, as an insult. Foma Fomitch had to be somebody from the days of Stalin, of Beria.

The secretary took down every history of the Party and of the Soviet Union he had on his bookshelves, and looked in the indexes for the name Foma Fomitch. It was not there. He checked in the index of Gramsci's *Notebooks*; he searched in every book that dealt with Communism and that had a proper-name index. To no end. He bethought him of Czechoslovakia, of what had happened after the Prague spring, but in the newspaper accounts there was no name that even resembled Foma Fomitch. He phoned the Honorable di Sales, a man who was widely informed and of formidable culture. That name, the Honorable di Sales said, he had read or heard that name somewhere, but where or when he could not say; he could not remember. The secretary then telephoned the office of the regional federation and asked to speak to the comrade who was in charge of cultural affairs, a man who had been to Russia many times. The cultural-affairs comrade wished to be informed of the context in which the name had come up. The secretary informed him in minute detail. "As for the name's being Russian, it is Russian. I can also tell you that it means Thomas the son of Thomas. . . . I'll see what more I can find out." Thus the name traveled across telephone wires and reached Party officials who had spent vacations in Russia as well as members of Parliament who had long sojourned there in exile. It seemed to all of them that they had heard or read the name, but they did not remember when, they did not remember where. The secretary moved on to teachers and scholars of history: they were very sure that they had never heard or read the name. Finally, after two days, a professor of Slavic literature solved the mystery: the name occurred in a humorous novel by Feodor Dostoevski, *The Friend of the Family*, 1859. Was there an Italian translation? There was, the professor replied when questioned again. It had been published in 1927, in Turin. The secretary implored the regional-federation man to secure a copy for him. It would be useful to him, he said, in preparing the motion to expel that rapscallion from the Party, that whippersnapper who had made so many people lose so much time chasing after Foma Fomitch. The regional federation sent him on a copy. The secretary read it in a fury. A humorous novel, a comic character: that Munafò would pay for this.

Some word of the feverish search leaked out. And then, at the meeting called to ride Candido out of the Party, the secretary spoke at length about the character, saying that he did not recognize himself in that person and that a Communist who saw a Foma Fomitch in the secretary of the cell to which he belonged was beyond doubt unworthy of being a Communist. Thus the nickname Foma Fomitch stuck, and since the secretary has made his way up in the Party, to this day he is known by that name, even by comrades in other cities.

While the name was being efficiently, tenaciously pursued by the Party, Candido and Don Antonio were discussing and arguing about the Dostoevski character. In this sense: Candido sincerely saw the great Party, from which he was surely about to be expelled, as having degenerated in its leadership to so many Foma Fomitches, of whose character he took the same dim view as had Dostoevski—a do-nothing, a good-for-nothing Tartuffe. While Don Antonio agreed that the Party cadres might be made up in part of Foma Fomitches, he did not view the character, hence the Party characters who resembled him, so negatively: Dostoevski, Don Antonio said, *malgré lui* had given the character a charge of positivity, of positive effectiveness, positive action; by way of example, he adduced the scene in which Foma Fomitch prevails upon the Colonel to address him by the title "Excellency," a title that was not due him. It was, yes, a disturbing novel, notwithstanding the tag of "humorous," which the author had applied to it: disturbing in the sense that one could take it as a prefiguration, an advance warning of one possible destiny of the Communist Party, of all Communist parties—of a Communist world; but if one wanted to see it in this way, one had to be consequent, as the novel is consequent, and recognize that in the end Foma makes everyone happy.

"Yes," Candido said, "but everyone could have been happy before, without Foma." One could not say that, Don Antonio replied. Happiness that is easily won at first is not the same as happiness that is hard won later; something one enjoys unawares, without first having suffered, one cannot even call happiness. Candido objected that a maxim like that had nothing to do with Marxism; Don Antonio admitted that no, it did not have anything to do with Marxism, but with life, with man, yes. Returning to Foma, he said that one could perceive in the character—in how he arouses inhibitions, fear, and self-criticism in Stepantchikovo—a kind of prefiguration of Stalin and Stalinism. However, Candido did not entirely agree with this: about Stalin, no, but about Stalinism after Stalin, yes, about the Stalinism of de-Stalinization, yes. Considered in this light, the analogy between novel and historical reality was exact, flawless: de-Stalinization had originated with people who had feared Stalin so much that they made him laugh, people whom Stalin had reduced to the rank of court jesters; and Foma Fomitch, as Dostoevski describes him before introducing him to us, was a little despot who had emerged from the skin of a jester, which was what he had been earlier for the deceased General Krahotkin.

"You are a Stalinist," Don Antonio said. When Candido was about to protest: "No, I don't say that as a criticism. After Bonaparte, there were people who happened not to have been Bonapartists and those who never would have been —which is to say, the best, which is to say, the young. . . . You do not concede that one can compare Stalin to Foma Fomitch, but the difference between them is purely quantitative and, so to speak, of a literary nature: many many more victims—definitively victims—for Stalin; for Foma, only a few, their suffering brief, their lives destined to end happily. Tragedy, comedy . . . But look here: Stalin stood in relation to Marxism the way Arnobius stood in relation to Christianity. Both had vast—total—scorn for man, for humanity; a gigantic pessimism. Arnobius believed salvation could be had only through grace, since man's strength was insufficient for him to attain to goodness. And the same with Stalin, except that Stalin's grace was the police—a grace that manifested itself, let us say, by exclusion, whereas Arnobius's did so by inclu-

sion. Stalin's grace graced only those whom it did not touch.
. . . And I should say I am not thinking of Arnobius without
cause. . . . Do you know who has written most vividly—
I could also say most movingly—about his seven-book
Adversus nationes? Concetto Marchesi. And Marchesi is the
most vigorous—or at least the most overt—Stalinist our Party
has tolerated since the Khrushchev report."

" 'Our' Party," Candido echoed, with bitter irony. "You
might better say 'my' Party, since they're surely going to
throw me out."

"Eh, yes, my Party . . . Because, you see, I have to stay
in. To unfrock myself twice in the space of a few years would
be a little too much."

"I know. . . . Let's go back to Stalinism. It's a subject that
interests me," said Candido.

"Let's go back to it," Don Antonio said. And he added
ambiguously, "We will always be going back to it."

About the disappearance of Paola, and about
what she forgot to take with her

Candido was thrown out of the Party; the vote was almost unanimous, since only Don Antonio did not raise his hand. He did not raise his hand not only because he knew Candido and loved him but also because that method of voting against someone greatly resembled casting a stone; therefore, he would never have raised his hand against anyone. When he gave these as his reasons to the people sitting behind the table, who had observed him during the voting, he received in return a pitying smile and a witticism—the Bible had nothing to do with the Party.

Candido did not take it too hard. He maintained that he was a Communist without a party, against Don Antonio, who argued that it was impossible to be a Communist outside the Party. And indeed, Candido did lack, had come to lack, something. But he still had Paola, the friendship of Don Antonio, his farm work, his books. Paola, on the other hand, seemed more affected by Candido's expulsion than Candido. She blamed herself. In spite of Candido's telling her that his being out of the Party did not matter to him, she fretted, she seemed to grow more and more dissatisfied with herself, gloomy, almost sullen. Sullen with Candido, on whom, she said, she had brought down this first small disaster, which could be followed by other, larger disasters. And so, by dint of imagining disasters, she ended up creating the conditions whereby they might come to pass.

Returning from the fields some months after his expulsion from the Party, Candido did not find Paola at home. He found a letter on the kitchen table: "Dear Candido, I am going away. I don't want to go on causing you harm. A woman like me is better lost than found. I love you very much. Paola."

There was a postscript: "I'm taking some things that I know you don't care about. They'll be useful to me in going back to face a life that without you will be hard and very unhappy."

Candido wept. He wept the whole night long, he wept the next day, he wept all the days he spent shut up in the house, wandering about, touching things that she had touched every day. He drank coffee, he continued to weep, and now and then he fell into a sleep that was not sleep but a dolorous, delirious stupor. On the third or fourth day—he had lost count—Don Antonio came, worried not to have seen him. Wordlessly weeping, Candido showed him the letter.

Don Antonio embraced him. He found no words in the face of that grief. The first words he presently did find were, however, these: "What did she take off with her?" Candido waved his hand in a gesture as much as to say, I don't know and I don't care; it also bespoke impatience with the shabby question. Don Antonio was mortified. "Even if later in life you choose poverty," he said, "even if you invite it and find it a cause for joy, when least you expect and would want it the poverty you knew as a child comes out in meanness and wickedness. . . . At this moment I am being mean and wicked because I want to discover that the person who is making you suffer is mean and wicked. . . . Or perhaps I want to make a count of what she took with her so that you will suffer less. . . . I don't know, I am floundering even inside myself. . . . But the fact is, I want to know: What has she taken with her?"

94

Candido would have liked to answer that she had taken everything with her, that she had taken his life with her. He was about to say this. But he was ashamed, as if sensing it was a lie: for in one part of himself, at the moment small and dim behind the harsh and enveloping glare of his pain, he felt his love for life like a firm, tenacious root which would branch out beneath that field of pain. In a flash, he even doubted his own grief, as if it were sham, yet strong enough, albeit a sham, to become part of a character of innumerable unified elements.

"What did she take with her?" Don Antonio asked again.

Candido began to open doors and drawers automatically, swiftly, looking almost without seeing. He went back and sat down in the armchair in which he had been sitting for three or four days. Guessing rather than knowing, despite the survey just completed, and to satisfy Don Antonio's curiosity, he said, "She took some money with her, some gold jewelry, maybe the silverware, too." He sat staring at a point behind Don Antonio's shoulders so long and with such an inscrutable expression that Don Antonio turned to look. There was a console table, on which stood two silver candelabra.

"The candelabra," Candido said. "She forgot the candelabra. They're very old, they're worth more, perhaps, than all the other things she took. . . . I'll see that she gets them."

Good Lord, Don Antonio thought, how false real things are. Here we are, back with Monseigneur Myriel, Jean Valjean, *Les Misérables*. Or is our life nothing but what has already been written? . . . We believe that we're living, that we're real, yet we are merely the projection, the shadow of things already written.

Candido sensed Don Antonio's thought, and the recollection of pages he had read not many years before opened for him.

"I'm playing a part," he said. "Or perhaps I'm beginning

to despise her. The idea of seeing that she gets the candelabra came to me, I know now, from something between sham and scorn. It was not a loving thought. Even before, when I was reading *Les Misérables*, I thought that Monseigneur Myriel was going beyond love, that his love was spilling over into scorn. . . . You knew very well what you wanted when you asked me what she had taken with her. You wanted to make me miserable. . . . Well, I am miserable. Are you satisfied?"

"No, I am not satisfied. The impoverishment is mine, truthfully. . . . And I want to tell you one thing that perhaps will make you suffer more: I am convinced that she took what she took with her only to savage the image you have of her, so that you would despise her. . . ."

"Now we come to the melodrama," Candido said. Then, after a long silence, he said, wearily, "But things are always simple." He closed his eyes. After a bit, Don Antonio realized that he was sleeping—heavily, hardly breathing.

When Candido opened his eyes again, he believed that he would find Don Antonio standing in front of him, and that he would have to explain why things are always simple and why what had happened to him was simple; but hours had passed, and Don Antonio had gone away.

Candido felt hungry. Hunger was quickened in fantasy: bread fresh from the oven, spaghetti fragrant with garlic and basil, sausage dripping its fat on the embers. He found some stale bread and some butter, and began to eat it without appetite. His grief was now a quiet phantom, as if it had issued forth from him and was hiding in the dark and silence of the house.

Candido talked with the phantom, with Paola, with Don Antonio, with the secretary of the Party, with the universe. He actually talked aloud and, as if divided in two, he listened to himself. It was like a delirium; if one could express it in visual terms, his delirium was like the ruins of an ancient building, no piece of which is missing, yet each piece must be raised, one by one, and juxtaposed. A task for which we are poorly suited, not loving ruins of any kind. We can say simply this: that from the fragments of his and Paola's love story, which Candido told over and over to himself, there remained a sense of joy, of happiness, which the ending—Paola's flight, the way in which she fled—did not disturb or muddy. That Paola had gone away, sacrificing her love for him or freeing herself of him, had no importance. The fact was, she had gone away, and only facts count, only facts should count. We are what we do. Intentions, especially if good, and regrets, especially if just, each of us can play with inside ourselves as we wish, to the point of disintegration, of madness. But a fact is a fact; it is without contradictions, ambiguities; it does not contain what is different, what is opposite. That Paola had gone away signified one thing only for him: something had happened between them which had shattered the harmony of their living together, the delight of their bodies. A fact. To question, to interrogate, to examine would have availed nothing except to complicate painfully all that had been simple and true. They had met in the truth of their bodies, and in that joyous truth they had lived together. Then, perhaps, the body of Paola had given way before her spirit. Before her immortal spirit, emotional spirit, beautiful spirit; and the joyous truth of the body had dimmed for her, had been distorted, had become an inferior good. Temptation, untruth: as in the Book of Genesis. Except that the temptation had been the spirit, whether immortal or emotional or beautiful. It is the spirit that lies, not the body. "Our body is the good dog that leads the blind." And on this thought, which had come to him clear and helpful among his own frenzy and confusion, as the thoughts already thought by others always are clear and helpful at moments when our own vacillate, Candido again sank into sleep.

*About the decision that Candido made to
free himself of his land, and to travel, and
about how his relatives went to great pains
to set him free*

For Candido, without Paola time was as stationary and hard as a rock, as if it were contracted and hammered into the present; had he tried to turn it around, nothing would have appeared but the past. There was his work, there were his books, there were the conversations with Don Antonio, but everything was repetition, boredom, pain.

Candido decided that he must make something of himself, of his life; he must bestir himself in order to try to stir the love of life within him which he felt he had not lost.

He spoke of this first with Don Antonio, who approved. Then he went to speak to the secretary of the Party, who had had him thrown out. He told him he had decided to turn his land over to the Party, to a co-operative of peasants and trained agriculturalists which should be set up within the Party. He did not know how, what formalities, what legal steps were needed; but let the Party people look into it, since they had formed so many co-operatives in northern Italy.

The secretary listened to him with an icy sneer. Then he said, "So who do you think you are? Tolstoy?" This was his most immediate revenge against Dostoevski, to whom Candido had had recourse in the general meeting, and against the mysterious Foma Fomitch, whom Candido had evoked and whose name—as now he knew—had become his nickname.

Candido was not expecting such a witticism. Because he felt not a shadow of bitterness toward the secretary, he would never have imagined that the secretary might feel any toward him. He blushed, and felt as if he were at fault. The secretary, however, believed that he had touched him to the quick, and that Candido would only hate him more since he supposed himself already hated for the expulsion business. Therefore he became more logically aggressive. He said, "Point Number One: Where am I going to find peasants to form a co-operative? The few who are still here prefer to work by the day on other people's land. I would never be able to convince them to try an experiment like a co-operative. For one thing, they distrust each other and you and me and God Almighty. . . . Point Number Two: supposing that conditions did exist for accepting your proposal, I would get into an endless judicial tangle, and I'd get the Party into it, too. And we wouldn't look good, either the Party or me. People would say, and they'd be right, that we took advantage of an imbecile. . . . Point Number Three: playing tricks with me is a waste of time. The man who can get yours truly into a mess has yet to be born, and perhaps never will be born."

"Who is an imbecile?" Candido asked. "Who is it who wants to play tricks?"

"You, my friend."

"An imbecile? I want to play tricks? . . . Why? How?"

"The why and the how you know very well."

"I swear to you I don't know, and I don't understand." He spoke with such desperation that the secretary, thinking he might indeed not know and might not understand, became convinced that he really was an imbecile.

"Don't you know that your relatives have started proceedings to have the court declare you mentally incompetent?"

"What does that mean?"

"It means they want to get their hands on everything you've got."

"I didn't know that," Candido said.

"If you didn't know it, that's one story," the secretary said. "But if you did know, and if you came here so that the Party and I would walk into the trap of taking on your case against your relatives, defending you against them, vouching for your mental health, that is another story, and you've got that story all wrong."

"I didn't know," Candido said. "And please excuse me—but only for having made you waste your time, *not* for having tried to trick you, because I didn't try."

He went to Don Antonio and told him everything. Don Antonio flew into a passion—against the secretary, and even more against Candido's relatives. But Candido was stung more by the fact that the secretary had believed him capable of plotting a deception than by the fact that his relatives wanted to have him declared mentally incompetent. On the contrary, he felt almost relieved, comforted, by the fact that his relatives were seeking—albeit in their own fashion and in their own self-interest—a solution to his problem of how to free himself of his land, of his possessions. He had taken great interest in his land, he had worked on it, but with no sense of proprietorship, of possession, as if cultivating the land in the best possible way, making it more productive, more ordered, tidier were a part of right living and had nothing to do with money. It was something akin to love. Love for Paola. And now that Paola had gone away, his daily labor seemed to him degraded: it was drudgery, nothing but drudgery throughout the unchanging course of the seasons, the way it had always been for the peasants, who were never content, always cursing the rain or the sun, the hail or the frost, the phylloxera that attacked the vines, or the smut

101

that attacked the wheat. The truest allegory of life was what the countryside spread daily before the peasant's eye: toil lying in wait for him daily, toil brought often to naught; diseases that arose invisibly and spread inexorably. And even those diseases as named by the peasants were an allegory of life: red rust, black rot, white blast.

Candido's indifference to his relatives' maneuvers to have him declared mentally unfit did not sit well with Don Antonio. He could not even conceive how anyone would so calmly let himself be stripped of what was his—no matter how unjust property was, no matter how unjust the laws that protected it. . . . And to be certified an imbecile into the bargain! Therefore he promptly busied himself to inquire into the maneuver: exactly who among Candido's relatives had initiated the action; on what allegations the petition was based; who was the lawyer, and who the judge; at what point did the matter stand in the judicial labyrinth; and what did the judge think of it. He knew everything in a matter of days.

The brothers and sisters of Candido's father had always hoped, as we know, to get their hands on their brother's estate; that is, to carry out Francesco Maria Munafò's intention to disinherit Candido, which the lawyer would certainly have put into effect had he had time. But blocking their hope there had been, first, on Candido's side, the General: a man with powerful connections because of a past that was not past and because of a present that resembled the past. When the General became disgusted with Candido, and when Concetta got out and "that woman" got in, their hopes rose. But another impediment had been created by Candido's joining the Communist Party, which at that time would certainly have helped and protected him.

Candido's expulsion from the Party was a signal to them that the way was clear. They assayed the feelings of the

General and Concetta. The General did not want even to hear of Candido, while Concetta wanted not only to *hear* talk of him but also to talk of him as the unhappy creature whom she had brought up at the price of twenty years of love and sacrifice, and who was now rushing toward an unhappy end. Nor did they neglect to assay public opinion, which was unanimous: a woman like Paola "would have eaten him alive" through the *ars amandi* in which she was undoubtedly most expert and through her greed for money, which in such a woman as she must be strong and ruthless. But while they were preparing the petition, Paola ran away. Since it was known that she had gone off when Candido was not at home, carrying with her very heavy valises, the suspicion that "that woman" might be robbing Candido became a certainty: she had robbed him.

Don Antonio succeeded even in getting a copy of the petition. By way of a general demonstration of Candido's mental deficiency, two facts were set forth which, because the document strove so hard to be subtle, were self-contradictory: one, Candido was a big landowner, yet he had joined the Communist Party, which, as everyone knows, wants to hand all land over to the peasants; two, because he displayed an exhibitionistic mania for giving away his land, after about a year the Party had very wisely expelled him. The document then proceeded to a more detailed enumeration; among the items were Candido's offer to donate gratis to the community a considerable parcel of land, valued at several million lire; the insane expenditures he had made to bring highly questionable improvements to his land; his cohabitation with a woman of unknown origins, who had performed the most humble function in the house of his grandfather—said cohabitation considered scandalous by the woman who had brought him up (Concetta Munisteri, fifty-one years of age, now in the

103

service of the Honorable Arturo Cressi: to appear as witness),
and deplored by his grandfather (General, now the Honorable
Arturo Cressi: also to appear as witness), said cohabitation
terminated by the flight of the woman from the Munafò house,
she presumably—as everyone in the city presumed—carrying
with her objects of value from the Munafò patrimony.

"Beautiful!" Candido said. "With a petition like this, they're
bound to take the land away from me."

About the colloquy that Candido had with a
judge and a psychiatrist, and about the judgment
of mental incompetency that followed from it

Aunts and uncles—the aunts with their husbands—were seated in a row in the judge's anteroom. Six, plus their lawyer, in so small a room constituted a crowd. Candido greeted them cheerfully. Suspicious of that cheer, they responded coldly. But one of the aunts added to their group greeting: "We are doing this for your own good."

"I know," Candido replied, thinking that the aunt and all the others really were convinced it was so. So many things are done for the good of others that become bad for others and one's self. Thus Paola had gone away. Thus these people wanted to save his property for him—or if not to save it for *him*, at least to save it. Property, the Munafò patrimony: a kind of abstraction over which they would eventually tear each other to pieces.

They were called into the judge's chamber first. Elbowing their way, they rushed in almost as if there were not room for all and the last feared they might remain outside. They were there for almost an hour; they came out less gloomy, almost pleased, and most pleased of all was their lawyer. They bade Candido good-bye and swarmed out. From the door to the judge's chambers, the clerk called, "Candido Munafò," and Candido crossed the threshold of the office. Behind a writing desk sat the judge: a hard face unnaturally open in a smile, hair thick and black over a low forehead. To his right, but as if apart, sat a very thin man, with staring eyes; the fingers of one hand kept nervously, continuously combing his untidy hair. Behind a smaller desk sat the clerk.

The judge half rose to shake Candido's hand, and presented —"Dr. Palicatti"—the gentleman who sat on his right and who blinked by way of greeting. With a wave of his hand, the judge invited Candido to sit down facing the two of them. The judge looked at him closely. Dr. Palicatti gazed at him with dull, absent eyes.

"Well, now . . ." the judge began. "Well, now . . ." He shuffled some papers, he touched pens and pencils, and seemingly among them found words to append to the "well, now." . . . "Well now, as you know, your relatives wish to have you declared mentally incompetent. . . . What have you to say about that?"

"Nothing. You are the one who must say something about it to me."

"Correct. It is I who must say something about it. . . . I, and Dr. Palicatti . . . Dr. Palicatti," he explained, "is a psychiatrist."

"Ah," Candido said. He was not expecting that, but he should have expected a psychiatrist would come into the case.

"And so," the judge resumed, "you have nothing to say about this action of your relatives to have you declared mentally incompetent."

"I can say that it is lunacy on their part to take on themselves the burden of minding my property."

"Lunacy, you say." The judge seemed satisfied. "Lunacy . . . Very well . . . What would you think of that, Dr. Palicatti?"

The doctor raised his right hand in a gesture that could be condemnation, absolution, expectancy, indifference.

"In sum," the judge continued, "you do not consider it reprehensible on the part of your next of kin to take the management of your estate out of your hands?"

"From a personal, egoistic point of view, I even consider it a good deed."

"You hear that?" the judge asked the doctor. His satisfaction was now expressed in a sneer.

"I hear it, I hear it," the doctor said, with some irritation.

"But then," the judge asked, "why did you not, on your own, without waiting for matters to come to this point"— he ruffled the papers before him as if to mix them up—"offer your relatives the management of your estate, the care and safekeeping of it?"

"They didn't ask me to do so. And, also, I thought it would be asking too much."

"Ah, asking too much . . . Very good . . ." He turned an inquiring eye on the doctor, but, encountering a blank stare, he looked away.

"And then," Candido added, "the moment the law is involved—and they have turned to the law—it's better to do things in an orderly way, according to the law, according to justice."

" 'According to the law, according to justice' . . . That's beautiful," the judge said. "Beautiful." He sat absorbed, as if beguiled by the beauty of those two words, those two ideas: law, justice. Then he said, "So far as I am concerned, this will do. . . . Doctor, have you any questions to ask our friend?" The expression "our friend" and the tone in which he said it were proof to Candido that the judge considered him now fully deserving of the certification his relatives had requested.

"Many questions," the doctor said.

"Ask them," the judge invited.

"Well," the doctor said, "I should like to know something about your being expelled from the Communist Party."

Candido related the story in an orderly way.

"The certification of mental incompetence," the doctor said when Candido had finished his account, "I would award to the Communist Party."

"What?" The judge was taken aback. "Aren't you a Communist?"

"I am," the doctor said, "but, let's say, a bit *refoulé.*"

"Oh, good heavens . . . Chinese?" the judge asked, in consternation.

"Not exactly . . . However, don't be alarmed. I'll pass this case on to a colleague of mine who is a Social Democrat. . . . A conscientious man, a first-rate doctor . . . But all the same, Signor Munafò must go into the hospital for a few days for observation. . . . One can't just, off the top of one's head—"

"All right, all right." The judge cut him short. "We'll talk about that presently. Meanwhile, Signor Munafò, you may go."

And so it was that Candido spent two days in a lunatic asylum. He was well treated. But he almost went out of his mind to see how others were treated. And even if he did not go mad, he received from the first-rate, conscientious, Social Democrat doctor the certification of mental incompetence that the judge, his relatives, and he himself expected.

About the party that Candido's relatives gave him
as a reward for his behavior before the judge and
the doctors; and about the troubles that befell
his relatives as a consequence of that party

Of the facts that eddied around his certification, two remained indelibly significant in Candido's memory: Dr. Palicatti's withdrawal from his case, and the sudden, burning affection with which his relatives surrounded him once the certification of mental incompetence had been ordered by the court.

Dr. Palicatti was the first example Candido had come across of a Communist who stands to the left of the Communists. He had heard that there were such, but he had never met any. The ease with which the doctor, having made his quip about the Communist Party and aroused the judge's suspicions, had then washed his hands of passing judgment according to the dictates of science and conscience had made a tremendous impression on Candido. Later, in the hospital, he had seen the doctor, gone up to him, and introduced himself. "Ah, yes," the doctor had said, "I remember. . . ." As if five years, and not five days, had passed since they had met in the judge's chamber. "But my dear friend, I always wash my hands of these sordid cases. . . . Money, property . . . Do you suppose it matters to me whether they stay with you or go to your relatives? Destroy them, that's what must be done, destroy them—money, possessions, you, and your relatives . . ." and he strode off, furiously ruffling his hair. Candido was startled, especially by that "dear friend," which had echoed the "dear friend" uttered by the judge.

As for his relatives, it seemed to Candido that, because of the way in which he had consented to their petition and had, in fact, before judge and doctor confirmed it as fair, they had persuaded themselves that he loved them: struck by remorse that for all those many years they had had no love whatever for him, they were now anxiously bent on bestowing on him a modicum of love. And since Candido had told them of his decision to leave, perhaps never to return (a decision they enthusiastically approved in their hearts and hoped might hold), all the affection they felt they owed him for the past and would like to pay him in the future they decided to express and concentrate in one plenary, bountiful family reunion; almost a party.

Candido scarcely knew the relatives who now loved him so dearly. Two aunts, two uncles, the husbands of the aunts, the wives of the uncles, and a dozen girl and boy cousins. Then there were others, more distantly related. Candido mixed up names and faces, and suffered throughout most of the evening. Until, finally, from that crowd, which was like a pack of cards being constantly shuffled, came forth the lucky card, the one never to be confused with any other, the one to trust, as always happens to the timid and bewildered when they find themselves in numerous, unfamiliar company. His cousin Francesca, the daughter of his Aunt Amelia. She could not be called beautiful, but her eyes and smile were luminous. Intelligent, vivacious, quick in playful banter and in incisive judgment. She attached herself to Candido, and Candido to her, for the rest of the evening, which is to say until dawn.

As they were bidding each other good-bye, Francesca said

to Candido, "I want to come with you." She said it smiling, as if joking, as if poised to withdraw, to flee; but in her voice there was a tremulous, tearful note.

"Where?" Candido asked.

"Wherever." And when she said it, her face was serious, decided.

Candido went home, asking himself whether he was about to fall in love or whether he had already fallen in love. He resolved, no matter which, to hasten his departure. But the next day, as he was going out into the country, suddenly he heard added to the roar of his motorcycle that of another drawing nearer and nearer. Francesca was riding along on his left, her face pale and resolute, her hair streaming in the wind. "I love you!" she shouted. "Me too!" Candido shouted back.

They spent several hours together, walking through the countryside. A week later, they went away together.

For the parents of Francesca, for the uncles and aunts of Francesca and Candido, for the entire crew of relatives, it meant ruin and defeat. At first, all were as one against Candido: they agreed that from the day of his birth he had spelled bad luck for the Munafò family; that it would have been the better part of wisdom not to meddle with him and his property; that someone like him, born bad and grown worse, could only corrupt and destroy everything good and beautiful. . . . Then opinions began to diverge, the parties to divide. The parents of Francesca lowered themselves so far as to hope that the union of their daughter with Candido might be legalized and sanctified by a marriage; ergo that the certification of Candido's mental incompetence which they had labored so long to obtain might be rescinded. But others viewed matters differently: they did not wish to relinquish custody of his estate. Intrigues became heated. Sturdy antipathies developed. There were a few scuffles.

Candido and Francesca learned a little about this later, but it was like news from some faraway land, from some remote time.

About the travels of Candido and Francesca,
and about their long sojourn in Turin

Candido still had some of his money left, although he had spent much of it on his land. Money accumulated by misers flows out from many sides, many holes, and it requires the kind of avarice that is called prodigality for it soon to be dissipated on so many sides. Candido had spent money judiciously, even if his spending had been considered folly in the verdict of mental incompetence, and he had some still. He had already decided, before meeting Francesca, to spend it on travel. Francesca was of the same mind. Later, they would find work.

Francesca had always wanted to go to Spain; Candido, to France. They went to Spain and to France. And then to Egypt, to Iran, to Israel. But everything everywhere was debased in comparison to what they had imagined. Only Barcelona for its people and Paris on all scores were not disappointments. But the beautiful part of their travels was loving each other, making love: as if the essence of places became fantasy in their bodies; as if the fantasy, or the memory, of those places was their very bodies.

Of misadventures, mishaps, and misdirections they had none. Loving each other and loving everyone—waiters, taxi drivers, guides, beggars, slum children, Arabs, Jews—they felt loved by everyone in return. They also witnessed things they knew could and did happen, but which, read about in a newspaper, would have slipped from mind without a trace;

when seen, they remained indelible and symbolic. In Madrid, the day the anniversary of the civil war that Franco had won was being celebrated, they saw the Generalissimo, who looked as if he were nailed to a baroque tombstone (Candido remembered the photograph his grandfather kept in his bedroom), and at his side they saw, attentive and smiling upon the military parade that flowed by below, the ambassador from Mao's China. And in Cairo, as full of Russians as Rome of Americans, in a café full of Russians (technicians, it was said, although they always went about in groups, with the step and wariness of a military patrol), they saw Egyptian police arrest a student because, a waiter explained later, he was suspected of being a Communist. Communist China rendering homage to a victory of Fascism, Communist Russia aiding a government that threw Communists in jail: Who knows how many of these contradictions, incongruities, and absurdities there are in the world—Candido and Francesca used to say to each other—that escape us, that we don't see, that we want to let escape us and not see? Because when things are seen, they become simple, whereas we have a need to complicate them, to make complicated analyses of them, to find complicated causes, reasons, and justifications. But when one sees them, they are not complicated, and when one suffers them, even less so.

On their return to Italy, they wandered about to choose a city where they would live and find work. Candido liked Milan; Francesca, Turin. They decided to live in Turin. Don Antonio recommended them to an unfrocked priest and to a priest who was about to be unfrocked; the latter found a job for Francesca in a nursery school, the former a job for Candido in a repair shop. They went to live in via Garibaldi, which was full of Sicilians. It was like finding their own country again. And they also found the Communist Party again, thanks to the two priests. It was very different from the one in their home city. Here in the North, the Communists knew everything about Communism. But it was a knowing everything that ended by being a knowing nothing. There in the South they knew nothing, and it was as if they knew everything.

Candido did not conceal the story of his expulsion from the Party; he recounted it in detail to the comrades in Turin. Those who heard the story made the comment that down there in Sicily everything could happen and everything did—even, unfortunately, in the Communist Party. They said that, with time and, of course, with the consent of the comrades who had expelled him, they would readmit him. But with time they began, instead, to mistrust him.

It all started one evening when they were discussing the danger of a coup d'état in Italy. They all believed it would take place, and no one except Candido put forward a doubt about its being successful. Someone said that they must keep themselves in readiness to leave Italy, and almost all declared themselves in agreement with that. Candido asked, "Where would you go?" Most answered that they would go to France; others, to Canada or Australia. Candido asked, and he also asked himself, since, like most of them, he, too, had thought of France: "How is it that none of us wants to go to the Soviet Union?" Some looked at him in a surly fashion, others grumbled. "Is it or isn't it a socialist country?" Candido pressed further. They answered, almost in a chorus, "Of course . . . For sure . . . It's a socialist country, of course." "Well, then," Candido said, "we should be wanting to go there. We're socialists." There was a chill silence; then, as if it were later than usual, and instead it was more than usually early, everyone got up and left.

A few days later, Candido learned from a comrade more

charitable than the others that, because of his remark that evening, the comrades now considered him a troublemaker. The more he tried, later, to explain, to clarify, the more they closed ranks behind their distrust and resistance. Candido was upset and embittered. Until one evening, coming home from a meeting, Francesca said, "What if they were simply imbeciles?" And that was the beginning of the liberation, of the cure.

Meanwhile, Turin was becoming a more and more sullen city. It seemed confusedly split, divided into two cities that were neurotically laying siege to each other, neither recognizing the other's positions, barbed-wire defenses, outposts, Trojan horses. The North and the South of Italy seethed there; they sought crazily to avoid each other and, at the same time, to strike out at each other; both were bottled up in producing automobiles, a superfluous necessity for all, a necessary superfluity for all. Literally bottled up: Candido applied to the city the metaphor of the two scorpions in the bottle, in which a well-known American journalist had synthesized the situation of the two atomic powers, the Soviet Union and the United States. The North and the South of Italy were also like two scorpions in a bottle—in the bottle that was Turin.

He wrote to Don Antonio about what Turin was like. And Don Antonio replied that yes, certainly, it was a terrible situation, but that the Piedmontese had asked for it, and, therefore, it was only fair that they pay. We Southerners are paying, too, Candido retorted. Yes, but at a certain point we will smash the bottle, Don Antonio answered. He had become a bit left of left, a bit Maoist, a bit French Sixth of May. But he was still within the ranks of the Communist Party. To jump over it to the left, he used to say, is pure,

116

boundless, circular folly: you would find yourself on the right before you knew it. But, Candido asked, isn't it like being inside another bottle? Yes, Don Antonio replied, but in one without scorpions.

About the trips of Candido and Francesca to Paris,
and about their decision to settle there

They used to go to Paris often, every time they had a holiday as long as four days, for that meant they could be there for at least three full days, taking into account the time needed to travel by train. They did not own a car. They had, naturally, decided against one since they lived in the city from which cars overran all of Italy. Among the reasons they loved Paris —besides those of love for love, love for literature, love for small and old things and for small and ancient trades—was that there one could still walk, still stroll, still wander aimlessly, still pause to look. Only in Paris, for example, did they walk holding hands; only in Paris did they move about at a delectably leisurely pace. In a word, there they felt relaxed and free. It was in their heads, yes, and it had to do with literature, but something about the spaces, about the rhythms of the architecture, and of the life moving through them agreed with the idea, perhaps a commonplace, which they had had of the city before knowing it. It was a great city, full of myths—literary, libertarian, and aphrodisiac—that trespass upon each other and merge; thus, in a Courbet nude one senses the interlude between one embrace and another, or between the Commune and a conversation with Baudelaire. But there was also a collectivity of small villages among which to choose, redesign and live what best appeals to us, what we were born to live or what we have dreamed of living. Little towns that facet and repeat the great city, a great city that smells of the country, that breathes in and nourishes itself on the country, and mirrors it through emblems. "Cats paused before the shops, waving their tails like flags. Like guard dogs, they stood with watchful eyes before baskets of salad greens and yellow carrots, cabbages of a purplish hue, and rosy radishes. The shops looked like gardens. . . . The outdoor cafés flowered with round tables on slender legs, the waiters had the look of gardeners, and when they poured the coffee and milk into the cups it seemed as if they were watering white flower beds. Trees and kiosks lined the curbs; it seemed as if the trees were selling newspapers. In shop windows, the merchandise fairly danced, but in a very precise and always supranatural order. The police strolled along the streets— yes, strolled—a raincape over the right or over the left shoulder; that such a garment should offer protection against hail or a shower was very strange. Nonetheless, they wore the capes with unshakable faith, whether in the quality of the cloth or the goodness of Heaven—who can say? They did not circulate like police but like people who have nothing to do, who have time to see the world." This was Paris for Lieutenant Franz Tunda in 1926 (Austrian, first missing in the war in Siberia, then in the peace in Europe), and so it was for Candido and Francesca a half-century later. Perhaps the city was no longer this for people who had been born and lived there or who had known it from before. "Paris is no longer Paris"—so say those who used to know the city well and those who do not know it at all. But for Candido and Francesca, Paris was still Paris.

And so they used to go there whenever they could, and they always longed to remain. In the shop, Candido often talked about it, and one day a comrade who was about to leave for Paris, to work there in the repair shop of a relative, proposed that he go along: the job was secure, the pay was good, and Paris was Paris. Candido talked with Francesca. Her instant enthusiasm was followed by worried second thoughts: Candido would find his own work again, but she would have lost hers. And how could they live in Paris unless she, too, worked and earned?

They were resigning themselves to give up when she got an idea; it came to her because she had been reading a book badly translated from French, and because she had been thinking about how badly translated it was. She had studied French at the Institute of the Sacred Heart, and she had never abandoned it; indeed, she had cultivated and improved her French. She went to the publisher Einaudi, and asked to be given a book to translate. In some perplexity, and rather to satisfy her and get her out of the way, they gave her to translate, as a test, *Un rêve fait à Mantoue*. Francesca glanced at a few pages. The name of the author, Yves Bonnefoy, was almost a greeting of good will. Goodfaith. The good faith. But the people who had given her the book to translate were not acting in such good faith. The text was difficult: so, they hoped to discourage her, to see her come back only to return the book and give up the job.

Francesca set stubbornly to work. She worked, one might say, day and night. When she went back to Einaudi, she knew everything about Bonnefoy that one could learn in the libraries of Turin, and she took with her one translated chapter. Presently they informed her that it was well done, that she could continue, and that her translation would be published.

Every evening, she would read Candido what she had translated. They both liked Bonnefoy, they almost loved him. *A Dream Dreamed in Mantua*. One evening, shortly before they were to leave for Paris and feeling as if they were caught up in a dream, Candido said, "Do you know what our life is, yours and mine? It's a dream dreamed in Sicily. Perhaps we're still there, and we are dreaming."

*About the correspondence between Candido and
Don Antonio, and about Don Antonio's
journey to Paris*

Don Antonio approved of their moving to Paris. He approved of almost everything that was born of restlessness, or that was an attempt to make what one wants or dreams come true. He approved of their move with the melancholy of the person who, himself a prisoner, does not envy the freedom others enjoy but only regrets not having seen, at a certain point in his life, the opening of a possible escape, a possible freedom. "I feel more and more the priest," he wrote, "and I am helped in this—a help I'd rather have done without—by the way the Party is evolving. I don't disapprove of it, I don't challenge it—a Marxism that does not evolve, that does not adapt to reality, that is not pliable, would be paralysis, a negation of itself—except in relation to me, to this self of mine that is long in dying and would like to be helped by others to die. . . . Perhaps I'll get married . . . or perhaps I'll become a priest again. . . ."

Sometimes he launched into outbursts of far-left ideas and invectives against the Party: "The Party of the working classes! And what's more—which is to say, what's less—the Party of an *employed* working class! As if an employed working class—precisely because it is employed, precisely because it therefore needn't worry—were not susceptible to corruption when it is woven into a rotten fabric as in fact it is. . . . Revolution can come only from *un*employment and from the schools, which are the immense antechamber of revolution. By this I don't mean *the* revolution, which by now has been postponed to some vague future, but the strength to make a genuine, effective change in Italian affairs. . . . However, the Party doesn't want to hear of the unemployed or of students —it wants to hear of them far less than they want to hear of the Party. The word 'students' makes a good Communist reach for his gun, like Dr. Goebbels when he heard the word 'intellectuals.' But I am not a good Communist." Yet at times he, too, reached for his gun: "What student leftists have not understood (and could not understand, since their ideas were spawned by the offspring of the middle class) is that you cannot tell a worker who at long last is eating three meals a day that precisely because he is eating regularly he is running the risk of not being revolutionary enough. The idea that he should leave his bowl of lentils to take up his revolutionary birthright does not seem one bit fair to the workingman. And so he sees in the friend who comes to him from the left, beneath all the revolutionary jargon, the red flags, and the portraits of Lenin, the old enemy who only yesterday came to him from the right."

Then Don Antonio reverted to quarreling with the Party: "Yesterday I met a boy who was just back from Moscow. He'd been sent by the Party and spent four months there, studying Marxism-Leninism—that is to say, Stalinism. Exactly the way one used to do twenty years ago. Today I asked the Honorable di Sales about it, and he said he knew nothing about it; on the contrary, he said, it seemed to him impossible. I gave him the boy's first and last names, and I described him. Di Sales knew who he was, but didn't know he had been sent to Moscow. Then he made a joke—a very open-minded joke. 'Perhaps,' he said, 'the dimwits are being sent there to school.' And I answered, 'Yes, that could be, but

since even in the Party the future belongs to the dimwits—'
He smiled and he was a little downcast. Perhaps he is convinced that the future does indeed belong to the dimwits,
since for some time now he himself has been kept on the
sidelines. Today when two Communists meet (but there must
be only two, not more), they talk about the Soviet Union,
about the Party, and about certain men in the Party with the
same freedom and nonconformism as when priests talk among
themselves about the Pope, the Roman Curia, or the episcopal
curia. . . . All the same, this story about the boy's being
sent to school in Russia means that all the fine talk about
Eurocommunism and Italian Communism and its emancipation
from the Soviet Union is just talk and no more. . . ."

Yet only a few months later he wrote: "To liquidate the
Stalin myth was already a big mistake; to liquidate the Soviet
Union myth is an even bigger one. For that matter, I don't
believe that the Soviet Union myth is an empty one (it is
for old-line Party people) or even that the Soviet Union is a
Fascist country, as some Communists are saying who still go
to Russia for medical care or endless banquets. After all, the
revolution took place *there*. . . ."

In his letters, Candido wrote about Paris, about his life
there with Francesca, about the things they were seeing. Don
Antonio, instead, wrote about nothing but the Party, about his
being a Communist, and about how the Communist Party was
or was not Communist. Each letter was the statement of a
single axiomatic truth. At one point, Candido tried to combine
all the truths. They did not hold together; it was like a
ferment, a spilling over. He wrote to Don Antonio: "I have
been rereading your letters. They express so many and such
conflicting truths that no one man can contain them all, nor
can one party." Don Antonio replied: "One party cannot
contain them all, and in fact, the Communist Party is carefully

choosing the worst. But the left can, and the man of the left can, yes. . . . These multiple truths must necessarily stand together, and together they constitute the drama of the left and of the man of the left. The Communist Party must go back to living them all if it does not want to move away from the left. . . . It's the same as the problem of free will and predestination for the Catholic: two truths that must coexist." Candido did not know much about the problem of free will and predestination. He replied: "What if the ensemble of so many truths amounted to one big lie? This is a simple question that could be given a simple answer."

Don Antonio answered: "We will talk about it when I come to Paris." Ever since Candido moved, Don Antonio had been saying that he would take a trip to Paris. After putting it off from one month to the next, from one year to the next, he did set forth, in August, 1977. Candido and Francesca met him at the Gare de Lyons. He had aged greatly; he was very tired, glassy-eyed, from the trip. But during the taxi ride from the Gare de Lyons to the Hôtel Saint-Germain, where they had made a reservation for him, just in reading the names of the streets and bridges, seeing the Seine and Notre-Dame, his spirits perked up, and he became once more the vivacious, curious, indefatigable Don Antonio of ten years before.

About the meeting of Candido with his mother,
and about the evening they spent together, and
about how, that evening, Candido managed
to feel happy

"In the evening I went to Lipp." It was like a refrain from a popular song, which came to Don Antonio's mind each time he passed by, and in the course of a day he passed by more than once, since the café was near his hotel. "In the evening I went to Lipp." Hemingway or Fitzgerald? Perhaps Hemingway: *The Movable Feast?*

Candido was with him once when, instead of repeating the phrase to himself mentally, he said it half aloud: " 'In the evening I went to Lipp.' " And Candido said, "This evening we will go . . . no, this afternoon, because in the evening it's hard to get a table."

They went in the afternoon. All the tables were taken, and they stood waiting for one to be free. Finally, they got one in a corner. It was uncomfortable for three, but Candido understood how, on the map of the mythical Parisian places which over many years of reading Don Antonio had drawn for himself, he would want to mark that place as visited.

Francesca and Candido ordered coffee; Don Antonio an armagnac, both because he could not swallow more than a sip of the coffee they make in Paris and because in Paris he wanted to eat and drink as the great books prescribe. Armagnac, then. Or pastis. Or calvados. Strenuous homage to literature for an almost teetotaling Sicilian, who was accustomed to drink no more than a half-glass of red wine with his midday and evening meals—like almost all Sicilians.

They talked about Hemingway and Fitzgerald, about Americans in Paris, about American writers whom Don Antonio had read during the years of Fascism and then thought very great, all of them, and whom Candido and Francesca had read later with indifference, even with impatience. An American couple was sitting beside them now. There was no mistaking their being Americans. The man's hair, above a plump, pink face, was very white and meticulously combed; he was wearing glasses with thin metal frames; he had a cigar clamped between his teeth. The woman's face was old, her hair white with violet tints; she wore large heavy glasses in the shape of a butterfly; her body was slender and youthful. In him there was something tired, bored, sleepy, in contrast to the volubility with which she was talking to him and moving her hands. Only American women are at once so old and so young, and only American men have that air of drowsy after-lunch fullness—a good after-lunch fullness, but verging on nausea—in front of their wives.

When Francesca, Don Antonio, and Candido sat down at the table near them, the woman was speaking and her husband was nodding, moving his head almost rhythmically. Then she fell silent; she seemed intent on catching what the three new arrivals were saying to each other. At a certain point, she turned to them and asked in Italian: "Italians?" Francesca, Don Antonio, and Candido said yes. "I'm Italian, too," the American said. There seemed to be nothing more to say, but after scrutinizing them at length, the woman asked again: "Sicilians?" When they responded affirmatively, she turned to her husband and uttered a long "Oh-h-h-h" of wonder and pleasure. It was the "Oh!" one hears Americans utter as they watch fireworks over the Seine on the Fourteenth of July; at each flowering of light in the sky, that "Oh-h-h-h!" winds like a thread amid the crowd to unite them all. "I'm Sicilian, too," she said then; and again she scrutinized them with a hesitant, anxious expression, almost as if the question she wanted to ask, that she was about to ask, must turn up her good-luck card.

Finally, she brought herself to ask it. "What city are you from?"

Don Antonio named their city.

She rose, tremulous with emotion, with agitation, her hand pressed to her breast as if to contain the beating of her heart. Speaking to Don Antonio but looking at Candido, she said, "You are Archpriest Lepanto, and you . . ." A few seconds earlier, Candido had known that this woman was his mother.

There ensued in Lipp a human-interest scene worthy of the tabloids, which ended when a waiter came over to their tables. They paid, they went out. Signora Maria Grazia took off her huge butterfly glasses and dried her tears. Tenderly supporting her and murmuring her name—"Grace, Grace"—her husband was looking at the three others with an air of disapproval, as if they were guilty of an intrusion that was spoiling his vacation.

Grace recovered her spirits. Pointing to her husband, she said to Candido, "This is . . ." Perhaps she was about to say "your father," perhaps "my husband." Her face turned red, and she became confused. After a moment, she said, "This is Hamlet." Hamlet shook hands warmly with Candido, with Francesca, with Don Antonio, asking each of them in Italian, "How are you?" All three replied that they were well.

For Grace and Hamlet, it was their last evening in Paris;

they were leaving the next day, nor could Hamlet delay their departure. It was a shame that they had met only on the very last evening. Candido was living in Paris; they had been there for two weeks: how wonderful if they had met earlier! But anyhow, that evening they would be together. Ceremoniously, Hamlet invited all three to dinner at a famous restaurant.

They walked about Paris, talking of their own city (which Hamlet considered was a little bit his, too, because for several months he had had it at his feet and because there he had met the woman of his life), about Sicily, about Italy, about Europe. Without doing so intentionally, they avoided talking of their own lives. But they were thinking about them, especially the son and the mother. Both made an effort to feel some love or remorse, yet had they been alone, they would have had nothing, or very little, to say to each other. Luckily, Don Antonio and Hamlet were there, and they had struck up a conversation about politics.

"After thirty-four years—" Don Antonio began.

"Just your age," Grace interrupted, looking tenderly at Candido.

"After thirty-four years," Don Antonio began again "perhaps I can ask you a question that I hope you will not consider indiscreet."

"Ask it," Hamlet said.

"Well, the question is this: How did you manage, only a few days after you had arrived in our town, to choose our worst citizens for public service? Did you just find them handy, or had they been pointed out to you in advance?"

"Were they the worst?" Hamlet asked, smiling.

"Yes, they were. . . . But mind now, I am asking you this out of, let's say, historical interest. There's nothing polemical about it at all."

"I can answer that. I don't think I'm still bound by any security regulation. I did not choose them. When they sent me to your city, they gave me a list of the people I should trust. . . . Must trust . . . In a word, those were orders." And very formally he added, "I'm sorry."

"We were far sorrier," Don Antonio said. "In any event, I always suspected as much. I mean, that you'd arrived with a list of the heads of the Mafia in your pocket."

"I'll tell you something. I suspected that myself; I thought they'd given me a list of mafiosi. . . . But we were fighting a war. . . ."

They talked about the war, about the peace, and about Germany. Grace and Hamlet had spent two months traveling around Europe, and only Germany had not disappointed them. "Europe," Hamlet said, "has become an orphanage: De Gaulle's orphans, Franco's orphans, Salazar's orphans, and in Italy, the orphans of the Communist Party. . . . The Germans are the only ones to have a father, even if he is a ghost."

"A ghost like the father of Hamlet for Hamlet," Don Antonio said.

Hamlet smiled at the reference. "But," he said, "since the only person in Europe to worry about all this is Sartre, does it seem to you that we Americans should have to worry about it? On the contrary, I think . . ."

They were already at the restaurant. "That's enough talk of politics," Grace ordered. "Let's think about dinner." Hamlet was knowledgeable about wines, chose them, and submitted his choice to the judgment of the others, but no one else was as knowledgeable as he.

They ate very well. Hamlet and Don Antonio drank copiously, the others moderately.

They accompanied Grace and Hamlet to their hotel. Grace

invited Candido and Francesca to move to America. "Some time or other," Candido promised, "we'll come. But as for living there, I want to live here. . . . Here you feel that something is about to end and something is about to begin. I'd like to see what should come to an end come to its end." Embracing him once again, his mother thought, He's a monster. But through her tears, she said, "America has everything. I'll be expecting you."

Candido, Francesca, and Don Antonio strolled down the Champs-Elysées. The night was mild, very soft. They decided to spend it walking through Paris, since the next day was a Sunday. All those good wines had not made Don Antonio what one could call happy, but they had freed him, fed his fantasy. He said, "You're right, it's true. Here you do feel that something is about to end, and it's beautiful. . . . At home, nothing ends, nothing ever ends. . . ." He uttered something like a sob.

They passed before the statues by Maillol. Don Antonio yearned to sleep beside one of those bronze women. "To sleep," he said, "to sleep chastely: the most chaste sleep of my life." He talked at length about chastity in the Latin of the Holy Fathers.

They passed the Pont Saint-Michel, and Don Antonio, almost preaching, began, "Here, in 1968, in the month of May . . ."

"Were they our grandfathers or our grandsons?" Candido interrupted.

"A disturbing question," Don Antonio said. And he fell silent. He was thinking, muttering.

From the quai they walked up the rue de Seine. In front of the statue of Voltaire, Don Antonio stopped, grasped the post of the street lamp, and bowed his head. He looked as if he might have begun to pray. Then, "This is our father!" he shouted. "This is our true father!"

Gently but firmly, Candido loosened his grip on the post, supported him, helped him on. "Let's not begin again with the fathers," he said. He felt himself a child of fortune, and happy.

Author's Note

Montesquieu says that "an original work almost always brings into being five or six hundred others which make use of the first approximately the way geometers make use of their formulas." I do not know whether *Candide* has served as a formula for five or six hundred other books. I believe it has not, unfortunately, because in that case we should have been less bored by so much literature. In any event, whether this story of mine is the first or the six hundredth, I have tried to make use of that formula. But it seems to me that I have not done so, and that this book resembles all my other books. That quickness and lightness can no longer be found, not even by me, and I do believe that I have never bored my reader. If not the result, then may the intention count: I have tried to be quick, to be light. But ours are heavy times.

Racalmuto, October 3, 1977

*Also by Leonardo Sciascia
in Harvill Paperbacks*

THE KNIGHT AND DEATH
Three Novellas
Translated from the Italian by Joseph Farrell and Marie Evans
"A first-rate storyteller with a pure style which carries his
narrative, sardonic wit and metaphorical undertow in its
deceptive, easy flow"
The Times

THE COUNCIL OF EGYPT
Translated from the Italian by Adrienne Foulke
"The Council of Egypt is the counterpart of *The Leopard*.
If *The Leopard* is a sumptuous semi-Proustian memoir of
pre-Risorgimento Sicily, *The Council of Egypt* is a chronicle
à la Stendhal from the era of the French Revolution"
GIANCARLO VIGORELLI, *Tempo*

DEATH OF AN INQUISITOR
and Other Stories
Translated from the Italian by Ian Thompson
"At Sciascia's death in 1989 the world mourned the passing of
a great writer. His books, however, are there for all of us to read,
and that should be cause of celebration"
GABRIEL JOSIPOVICI, *Independent*